Four Week Fiancé 2

Helen Cooper & J. S. Cooper

Thank you for purchasing and reading
Four Week Fiancé 2.
To be notified of any other new releases, please join
MY MAILING LIST.
http://eepurl.com/bpDQvz

Dear Reader,

This book was truly a work of love for you, for Mila and TJ, and for myself. Sometimes in our lives we are lucky enough to meet one person that truly touches our hearts and makes us want to reach for the stars. This book is for everyone that has loved and loved hard.

Jaimie
XOXO

Table of Contents

Chapter One

TJ

Five Years Ago

"HE'S SO HOT, SO DELICIOUS. I just want to melt into his arms." Mila was sitting on the couch, giggling on the phone as I walked out of the kitchen with two beers. I stood in the hallway and watched her as she lay back and rested her head on one of the bright yellow throw pillows that Mrs. Brookstone had adorning her bright green couch. Mrs. B. certainly didn't have the muted tastes of a Pottery Barn lover like my mother had.

"No, he does not want to do that." She rolled her eyes as she spoke, a huge grin on her face. "Sally, stop." She laughed again and I wondered what and who they were talking about. A small smirk graced my face as I wondered if they were talking about me. I clanged the bottles together by mistake and tensed as Mila realized there was someone in the room with her.

"What are you grinning at, TJ?" Mila's face darted to mine, her big brown eyes murderous as she saw me standing there.

"Nothing." I shook my head and held up my beer. "Just getting some cold brews for me and Cody."

"You'd better not be eavesdropping on me," she said, her voice weaker this time and her beautiful face red with embarrassment. So maybe she had been talking about me.

"I don't eavesdrop." I shook my head and walked towards her. Her long blond hair was tied up in a ponytail and she was wearing a pair of gym shorts with a white T-shirt—typical attire for a high school girl.

"Sure you don't," she said and licked her lips nervously. "Hey, Sally, let me call you back in a minute," she said quickly, putting the phone down on the couch and jumping up. "What do you want, TJ Walker?"

"To know how hot and delicious you think I am?" I asked with a small smile and winked at her.

"Ooh, you're a brute." Her eyes widened and she walked towards me with her hand out and punched me in the arm. "For your information I wasn't talking about you."

"Oh no?" I asked, my lips curling up as I stared at her heaving chest. I smiled at her again, my eyes teasing her, as she got all hot and flustered.

"No, I was talking about my boyfriend." She glared at me and I nodded.

"Sure."

"I was." She blushed and it was then that the doorbell rang. She hurried away from me to open the door and I saw some young punk standing there, reaching in and giving her a hug. The smile fell from my face as she hugged the guy back. Maybe she hadn't been talking about me after all. Maybe she'd been talking about this guy.

I turned away without a second glance and walked back to Cody's room. There were two reasons why I wasn't even going to let it bother me. One reason was because she was too young. I didn't date or do high school girls. The second reason was because she was Cody's sister. He'd flip a switch if I did any of the things I'd like to do with her.

I opened the door to his room and walked in and handed him his beer, my mind still on Mila, wondering what she was thinking about letting that punk do. I took a swig of beer and tried to get her off of my mind. One day, I'd have my chance and then she'd know just how scorching hot I really was.

Current Day

"MILA, I'M BACK." I WALKED towards her and smiled as she turned her head to look at me, her eyes wide and anxious. "Why do you look so shocked to see me back? Did you think I was going to leave you here?"

"I didn't know what to think," she said as she started to get up.

"Don't move." I put a hand up to stop her and shook my head. "We're not done yet."

"Where did you go?" she asked while she stood up. I had to smile at her disobedience, though I was slightly annoyed. To be fair, my annoyance was more born of fear. What if Mila had followed me downstairs and seen Barbie and my dad in his office? What would she have thought and said? The sinking feeling in my stomach told me that I knew exactly what would have happened next if she'd seen them.

"I went to get this." I held up the vibrator and showed it to her. I could see her looking at the object in my hands curiously and then she blushed as she realized what it was.

"Really, TJ?" she said and bit her lower lip as she looked into my eyes. "Being on a rooftop wasn't enough?"

"No." I shook my head and walked towards her, my tongue darting out of my mouth to lick my lips as I stared at her beautiful and enchanting face that gazed at me so excitedly, though I could tell she was trying to hide it.

"TJ, this seems dangerous."

"What's danger, really?" I asked, my question completely serious, though I didn't think she knew that. She didn't know that I was walking on a tightrope and that I was scared that my equilibrium was going to give at any moment.

"Danger is being perched on the side of a roof, practically naked. Danger is falling off said roof, naked. Danger is feeling like you're flying when you're perched on the edge of the world and you don't have wings. I'm not Icarus." She looked at me pointedly.

"Practically naked and naked are two different things," I said with a grin as I reached her and grabbed a hold of her hands. They were cold and slightly shaky and I realized that perhaps she was slightly scared of the situation we were in. "Are you scared?" My eyes narrowed on her face. "I don't want to do this if you're not comfortable."

"Who would be comfortable doing this?" she asked me, with a raised eyebrow. I stared back at her, and the teasing light in her brown eyes confused me. I wasn't sure what she wanted from me.

"So what do you want to do?" I asked, waiting for her answer. She licked her lips nervously and then pulled her hands away from me, gave me a small smile and walked back over to the ledge of the roof. I watched her get down on her knees and then she looked back at me, her long hair hanging over her shoulder as she gave me a sensual smile.

"I'm waiting," she said as she gazed at me. I stood there for a few seconds debating what to do. But then, I knew what I was going to do. I was going to make her believe that she had wings. I was going to make her soar. I wanted her to believe she could fly, yet, I was scared. What if my dad came to look for me? What if Barbie came with him? What if Mila saw them both? She'd have questions, demand answers I didn't want to give. Answers that I couldn't give. I felt something inside of me start to freeze cold with the position I was in. What was I really doing here? Why was I playing with this fire?

I could just walk away. Forget everything. Tell my dad no. Tell Mila I'd made a mistake. Tell everyone that everything was off. I didn't know how many times I could look into Mila's warm and hopeful brown eyes without crumbling. This wasn't what I'd expected. She was giving herself to me openly, her heart on her arm. This was something I'd not prepared for. Could she really be in love with me? I knew that she couldn't really be in love with me, not the real me. She didn't know who I was. Not on the inside. Not even really on the outside either. She only knew the side of me that she'd been shown. I was her brother's best friend. I was the handsome older guy who had been the subject of her dreams for many a year in high school. I wasn't sure about college and I hadn't even been sure about now until recently.

But now—now I knew that Mila had feelings for me, or at least thought she did. That was why she now found herself on top of a rooftop with me, waiting for me to take her.

My hand gravitated to her ass unconsciously. I felt my fingers running up her back, enjoying the feel of her slightly shivering skin, so alive and awake to me. I moved my fingers up higher and I could feel her heart beating through a nerve in her neck. *Thump, thump, thump*. Life that was breathing for me right now.

Her lips trembled slightly as she looked back at me, her expression curious as she waited to see what was going to happen next. I wanted to take her so badly. I wanted to bend her over, grab a hold of her hips and slide into her so hard that she wouldn't even remember what it felt like for me to not be inside of her.

I could do it so easily. She wanted me as badly as I wanted her. No matter how depraved the situation was she was still going along with it. She was going to let me fuck her on this rooftop. It excited me and sent such a thrill through my veins that I wasn't sure how I was able to resist her.

Her breasts glistened in the light, glowing at me, beckoning me in to touch her. Just one touch. My fingers caressed her nipple, and we both stilled. I leaned forward to kiss her, her lips soft and sweet next to mine.

"I'm ready, TJ," she said, swallowing slightly, her eyes open, wide, innocent.

"I know," I said and licked her lips before stepping back. "I know."

"What are you doing?" She frowned, looking at me with a perplexed expression. I watched as her brows furrowed and her lips turned up in an almost petulant expression.

I loved staring at her face. I loved looking at her expressions and trying to guess what she was thinking. Sometimes I just looked at her from across the room. It was something that I'd been doing for many years. Just watching her. Sometimes it was when she watched TV, sometimes when she was laughing with her friends, sometimes when she was arguing with Cody, and other times when she was talking to Nonno. I loved watching her with Nonno. It stirred something in me that I didn't really understand, but I loved to watch the two of them together; so easy, so relaxed, so loving. Sometimes she would crawl into his arms and he would rub her head and sing songs to her in Italian. She'd stare at him so adoringly and my heart would pause for a second. Then I would have to look away. I didn't want to be a creep, and watching her when she was in such a perfect moment always made me feel that way.

"I think this was a mistake," I said and pursed my lips at her. "We shouldn't have come up here."

"What are you talking about?" She got up off the ground and brushed off her knees, then took a step toward me. "This was your fantasy, right? You changed your mind?"

"I didn't change my mind." I shook my head, and wondered if my dad and Barbie had left the office yet. "I just don't think it's a good idea any more."

"Why not?" she asked me, her tone confused, offended and a little angry.

"It's just not something I want to do with you right now."

"So you'd do it with someone else, then?" Her eyes narrowed and

I tried not to smile at the hint of jealousy in her voice.

"Maybe." I shrugged, answering her honestly. I wanted to be as honest as I could with her, even though the entire situation was so far from honest, it wasn't even funny.

"Have you done it with someone else before?" Her eyes narrowed as she gazed at me and I could almost feel the palpable tension in her being.

"Why are we talking about this?" I asked her, annoyed. I didn't want to think about any other women. Not now. Of course there had been other women. Inconsequential women that had meant nothing to me. Not like her. I growled out loud as that thought hit me. She didn't mean anything to me. I mean, I liked her, cared for her, was attracted to her, liked to hear her laugh, loved to watch her smile, enjoyed smelling her scent, was addicted to the touch of her skin, soft and silky next to mine.

Yes, I felt more for her than I had the other nameless women I'd been with. But that feeling wasn't love or anything that could give her what she craved. I just wasn't that man. I was just bitter and jaded by life, love, and relationships, and as much as she meant to me, I just knew that ultimately I would disappoint her and it wouldn't work out.

"I guess I'm really special, huh?" she said, her face a twisted mask of hurt and slight bitterness. "How many women have you had up on this roof before me?"

"Mila," I said and grabbed her hands. "Please let's not go there. We're having fun here."

"We are?" She grabbed her hands away from me and shook her head. I watched as she gathered up her clothes and pulled them on quickly. "Let's just go. I want to go home."

"Mila, I'm sorry." I sighed, panic hitting me. What if we caught up with my dad and Barbie? "I mean, is there really any reason for me to tell you what I've done with other women in the past?"

"I was just curious." She sighed too and looked away, her whole body suddenly seeming to fall as if she was accepting some sort of inevitable defeat.

"Nothing in my past matters," I said honestly. "We shouldn't dwell on it."

"I'm not trying to dwell on anything. I just want to know. I just want to feel special," she said softly, mumbling her words so that I could barely hear her. My ears strained as I tried to concentrate on her words and my heart felt a pang of guilt. I was being selfish with what I was doing. I had to let her down gently. She had to know that this wasn't about her self-worth. I wanted more for her than this. More than *me*. Me and my fantasies and desires. She deserved better. Even though it killed me to think of her with someone else, smiling at someone else, touching someone else. No, I just couldn't think of it. When our relationship was over, I'd have to banish her from my life.

"You are special, Mila. You're the most special woman in the world." I grabbed her arms and pulled her towards me, holding her so close to me that I could feel her heart beating next to mine.

All of a sudden the EE Cummings poem, "I Carry Your Heart with Me," popped into my mind. *I carry your heart with me, I carry it in my heart,* I thought to myself as I closed my eyes and held her to me. I didn't want to think about what that meant. It was most probably because we'd been friends for years. She'd almost been like my younger sister. Someone to protect from the harsh realities of the world and someone to tease mercilessly.

"Make love to me, TJ," she whispered up at me urgently. "Make love to me so that we can fly."

"You want to fly?" I asked her softly.

"If you're the pilot, then yes." She looked up at me with an impish smile that tugged on my heartstrings.

"I'll be your pilot," I growled and leaned down and kissed her hungrily. She kissed me back eagerly and laughed as I licked her lips. I laughed back at her and I could feel my mood relaxing as I realized our awkward moment was over. The tension was gone from the moment and I could feel the excitement burning through my body again.

"You're so romantic, TJ, offering to fly me around the world," she said, teasing me. "Where will you fly me to first? Australia, England, South Africa, or maybe some cute little island in the Maldives?"

"You'd like that too much." I grinned down at her, feeling light-hearted. "I'll take you somewhere over the rainbow."

"Over the rainbow?"

"Yeah, somewhere no one else could ever take you." I winked at her.

"In a helicopter or a plane?"

"The only aircraft you'll be riding on is me." My hands reached down and caressed her breasts. She murmured slightly as my fingers pinched her nipples and my body reacted instantly. "I want you, Mila," I growled as my lips found her neck and bit down. "Oh, how I want you."

"Then take me," she breathed out, her eyelashes fluttering.

"Come," I said, grabbing her hands and bringing her to the edge of the roof again. "Kneel down again," I said and watched as she complied easily. I reached down and lifted her skirt up and touched her; she was already wet. Wet in anticipation for me. My body shuddered and I felt myself growing hard as I continued to touch her. "You want to feel me inside of you, don't you?" I massaged her shivering bud and I felt like a king. *I* had done this to her. *I* had her looking at me like she would die if I stopped touching her.

"Yes," she cried out as I pushed a finger inside of her. "Please, TJ, please."

I pulled her back up then and pulled her into my arms, kissing her softly before pulling her chin up to look at me.

"Do everything I say," I said steadily as she breathed heavily.

"Okay." She nodded, gazing into my eyes.

"I want you to hold this against yourself," I said as I handed her the vibrator. "I want you to hold it there and I want you to bring yourself pleasure, but you must not come."

"Okay," she said as she took the vibrator from me.

"I'll be very upset if you come."

"I mean, that's not something I can help." She giggled as she looked up at me.

"You only come for me," I said. "Your orgasms are for me and my cock."

"Jealous of a vibrator, TJ?" she said with a slight flush as she glanced at me.

"Jealous isn't quite the right word."

"What's the right word, then?"

"On your knees, Mila," I said gruffly. I placed my jacket and shirt down on the ground for her to rest on.

"So you just want me to hold it between my legs?" She looked up at me, clueless, and I couldn't stop myself from laughing.

"Hand it to me," I said and took the vibrator from her hand. I turned it on and then slapped it between her legs, holding it close to her bud. I moved it back and forth slightly, allowing my fingers to graze her gently.

"Oh my gosh, TJ." She squealed as she moved forward.

"Yes?" I whispered as I felt her growing wetter and wetter.

"I think I'm going to come."

"No, you're not," I said and held it there. "Not until I'm inside of you."

"I don't know what sort of self-restraint you think I have." She cried out. "But I don't think I'm going to be able to stop—oh, oh, TJ." She shuddered suddenly and I froze, wondering if she was going to come. I felt slightly put out. I didn't want her to come from a little plastic machine. I knew it was stupid of me, but I wanted to feel like only me being inside of her could make her come. I wanted to own her body. I wanted my cock to be her master. The secret to her pleasure.

"I want to feel you inside of me." She cried out again and looked back at me. "Please, now."

"Okay." I grinned and looked down at the pure lust and want on her face. It was enough to make my heart thump harder for a few seconds. She looked beautiful with her hair flying in the wind and her cheeks blushed pink. Her eyes looked dazed and her lips were trembling as she waited for me to take her. I pulled the vibrator away from her and she moaned. "No, baby," I said softly. "I want to make sure that when you come it's all because of me."

"Of course, it's all because of you." She cried out and I could hear the desire in her voice as she waited for her release.

"That's right, baby," I said, feeling cheesy as I said the words. I wasn't sure who I was becoming. I wasn't this man. I didn't get caught up. I didn't feel things when having sex. At least, not emotional things. I just fucked for a release. I didn't need to look into the woman's eyes, didn't care about wanting to see that look of pleasure and devotion in her stare as she came crashing down from her high. In fact, I hated it when a woman looked at me with anything other than lust. I didn't want her to feel that there was any sort of involvement aside from the sex. Because there wasn't.

That was different with Mila, though. I didn't know why. I didn't want to think about it too hard. She was just someone who'd been in my life for a long time and that was why it affected me differently. She was an innocent, not used to the games of men. I was going slowly, treading carefully because I cared about her feelings. I was still a bastard, though. If I weren't, I never would have taken her in the first place.

"Close your eyes," I said as I dropped down to my knees and pulled my pants down. My hands slid up in front of her and grabbed her breasts and pinched her nipples as I positioned her in front of me. My right hand fell from her breast and I guided my hardness inside of her. I could feel her quivering on me and it only made me grow harder. To know I had this power over her . . . that I could make her body come for me . . . that I could make her want me more than she'd ever wanted anything before. This was power. This was greatness.

"TJ," she screamed out as I pounded into her, hard, leaving nothing to chance. I slid in and out of her, guiding my cock as if commanding a great naval fleet. I stared out at the night sky as I felt her coming hard, screaming out my name, and as I felt myself withdraw from her and spurt onto the roof, I couldn't help but feel a sense of guilt, with my pride. This wasn't what it was about. This wasn't a moment to be proud of, though I couldn't stop myself from grinning down at her as she beamed up at me. My lips were smiling, but my eyes and heart felt dead. I had no idea what I was doing here, to her. All I knew was that I was in over my head.

Chapter Two

Mila

"WHICH ONE?" I HELD UP two dresses to Sally and frowned as she looked at them with an unimpressed expression on her face. "Too dowdy?"

"Not if you're going to Sunday school," she said, even-faced. "And you're teaching it. And you're the priest's wife."

"Ha ha, very funny." I rolled my eyes at her. "I don't know what to wear. This is the first time I'll be meeting the board of directors and the major shareholders. I don't want to let TJ down."

"I thought you met them already?"

"I met the board of directors, but not the shareholders as well." I sighed. "This is the first really, really important party. I'll be left alone. People will be asking me questions, judging me." I made a face. "I just don't want to let TJ down."

"Ask me if I care if you let TJ down." She pursed her lips and then smiled, a slow, totally innocent-looking smile. "I will help you pick a dress though."

"Hmm, what's the catch?" I narrowed my eyes as I gazed at her devious-looking face.

"What catch?" She grinned.

"Well, why are you so eager to help if you think TJ is a douche-bag?"

"Just because I think he's a douche, doesn't mean you do." She shrugged. "Plus, I want you to look so sexy tonight that he's not

13

going to want to keep his hands off of you, but he'll have to because this is a party with business associates."

"You're totally devious." I laughed at her. "But I like it. However, it can't be too sexy. Nothing that says I'm a hooker or a high-class escort."

"What about low-class escort?"

"Sally." I glared at her.

"Just joking." She giggled and headed to my closet. "Okay, let me see what you have in here." She rifled through my dresses and then looked at me. "I don't suppose he'll give you a credit card for a new dress?"

"He already gave me one." I made a face and sighed. "My wardrobe sucks, doesn't it?"

"He offered you a credit card?" Sally's eyes lit up. "To buy whatever you want?"

"I guess." I shrugged. "I didn't take it."

"You didn't take it?" Her eyes widened. "What are you? Dumb?"

"No, I already told you I don't want to give anyone any reason to think I'm a paid escort or whore."

"Who is 'anyone', Mila?" Sally shook her head. "Get that card and let's go shopping."

"Sally," I groaned.

"What?" She pulled out a flowery sundress. "Do you want to wear this or your slutty black Lycra dress that you got for the clubs?"

"Neither," I sighed.

"Exactly." She hung the dress back up. "You don't have a wardrobe for expensive dinners with millionaires. And tonight you need a dress that's going to wow the socks off of him. Tonight you have to give TJ a taste of his own medicine."

"Thanks."

"I don't have one either." She shrugged and then looked away. "And I most probably will never need one, either."

"Why not?" I said in my perfunctory way, though I already knew the answer would have something to do with her not having a boyfriend.

"Because I'll never be invited to those dinners," she said sorrowfully.

"Why not?" I asked and then continued. "Is it because you're going to be single forever?"

"Mila!" She glared at me.

"What?" I reached over and touched her shoulder. "You're not going to be single forever because my brother is a whore."

"How is he, by the way?" she asked softly, her eyes searching mine. I wasn't sure how to answer. Did I tell her that Cody had asked me about her twice now? Did I tell her that a part of me had a feeling that maybe Cody did like her, possibly? I didn't know what to do. She was my best friend, and as much as I wanted to make this better, I didn't know what to do or say. I loved her like a sister and I didn't want my brother to be the one to ruin our friendship forever, if he turned out to not like her or to like her and then cheat on her or something else crazy like that.

"I'm not sure." I shrugged and gave her a wry smile. "He's not really talking to me." I rolled my eyes.

"Why?" She looked at me with an expression of hope, as if she hoped that his reason for being so cold to me was due to the fact that she was my best friend and he wanted her.

"He said and I quote, 'you scarred me by sleeping with TJ. I'm not sure how I didn't lose it and rip you out of the bed, but I think shock stopped me. You should be thanking your lucky stars.' Ugh." I made a face at her. "He needs to just get over it."

"That is a big thing for him to witness, though." Sally laughed. "I mean, it's not every day you see your little sister boinking your best friend."

"True, ha-ha." I sighed. "I sure don't want to see *him* boinking

15

anyone."

"Not even your best friend?" Sally gave me a look and laughed slightly. She ran her hands through her hair and then sighed. "Why is this such a mess? I wish I could just not like him. I don't want to feel this way."

"I'm sorry." I reached my arms out to her. "I hate that you're feeling this way."

"It's fine." She made a face as I gave her a quick hug. "It's just what I get for falling for a guy who has never shown any interest in me."

"He has shown an interest." I stumbled over my words, trying to find a balance in telling my friend that she wasn't a fool, but not wanting to lead her on to thinking that he was interested. "But he's a player. I don't know how he's getting women because he sucks, but he's just not the 'settling down' type."

"Yeah, that's true." Sally's voice caught and I leaned back and looked into her eyes.

"You okay?" I asked, concerned by the tone in her voice.

"Yeah, I'm fine." She gave me a big smile, but I could see her eyes were still sad and looked wet.

"Oh, Sally." I stared at her. "You're not okay."

"I'm fine," she said, her lips trembling as she looked at me. "I feel like a fool, Mila."

"You're not a fool."

"I thought he liked me. I thought he was the one." Tears rolled gently from her eyes as she looked at me. "I thought he was my soul mate and that he just had to figure it out. I thought that deep inside he wanted me and he was waiting for the right moment."

"You never know," I said softly, not knowing what to say. I knew all too well what she was feeling. It was the same way I was feeling about TJ. My heart sank for the both of us, though I knew it would be selfish of me to bring up my fears and concerns regarding TJ in that moment.

"He doesn't give a shit about me." She wiped her eyes and laughed manically. "He fucked another girl while I was there. He wasn't even trying to hide it. I don't mean anything to him."

"Oh, Sally." I bit down on my lower lip, hating Cody for putting Sally through this.

"It's fine," she said again, maybe trying to convince herself. She took a deep breath. "I'm just PMS-ing." She made a face. "I'll be fine. It's not like we dated and he dumped me. We had nothing. Absolutely nothing. It's not his problem I liked him and was hoping for more."

"Sally . . . " I started, but stopped myself, not knowing what to say.

"It's okay, Mila." She grabbed a hold of my hand. "I'm sorry for being emotional. Let's figure out what dress you're going to wear tonight."

"Let's grab a glass of wine first," I said and headed towards the door so that I could grab a bottle of wine from the kitchen. "Wine and chocolate makes everything better."

"LET'S JUST GO TO THE store and have a look." I grinned at Sally as we sat across from each other and decimated a large bar of cookies-and-cream chocolate. "I might have enough to buy a new dress myself."

"Is that a request to borrow money?" she asked me with a raised eyebrow and a grin back, the chocolate having put both of our moods back up. "Exactly what money are you going to use to buy said dress?"

"Well, I have some." I laughed as my voice trailed off, my financial situation entering my mind unpleasantly. "Plus maybe I can get a store card."

"A store card?"

"Like a store credit card." I shook my head at her. "That way I have thirty days to pay it off, or more if they have a six-months-no-interest plan or something."

"Mila." Sally shook her head at me. "I've never heard that Valentino or Chanel had a store credit card and no, you're not getting yourself into more debt."

"I'm not really in debt." I laughed. "I just have no money."

"And you have a bunch of bills to pay each month." She rolled her eyes at me. "Where I come from, that's called debt."

"Where do you come from?" I said with a grin. "Wall Street? Bank of America Valley? Chase Street? Discover me discover you?"

"Ha ha, not." Sally smiled at me and sighed. "Mila, I know you don't like to think about these things, but you can't just be spending all your cash and charging what you can't afford."

"I'm trying to be good!" I exclaimed. "You're the one who told me to get a new dress."

"I know." She ran her hands through her hair and looked at me with a wry smile. "I got carried away, plus I figured that TJ could buy it."

"I just don't know how I feel about using TJ's money to buy stuff." I bit my lower lip. "It just seems to cheapen it."

"Cheapen what?" Sally looked at me cautiously. "You know that this isn't real, right? You're not his real fiancée. Just because he's fucking you doesn't mean he wants you for anything more than a good time." She stopped then and slapped her hand across her mouth as my face fell. "Forgive me, Mila. That came out a lot harsher than I'd planned. I guess I'm still feeling down about Cody and taking it out on everyone, like some sort of scorned bitch. I'm sorry, I didn't mean to take it out on you."

"Hey, I understand. And you're not a bitch," I said and sighed as we got up and walked back to my bedroom, having finished our glasses of wine and the entire bar of chocolate. I moaned loudly as we walked into the bedroom and I thought about all the extra calories I'd just taken in, and for what? I groaned and then fell down on my bed dramatically. "It's not like what you're saying isn't true. He hasn't given me any reason to believe that I mean anything real to him."

"I don't get guys." Sally plopped down next to me. "Why can't he see what he has right in front of his nose? Why can't he just smarten up and realize that you are the best girl for him? Why can't he just wake up and see that he loves you?"

"Yeah," I sighed and looked at her. "The same goes for Cody. Why can't he see that you're right here?"

"I wish I knew." She shrugged. "Maybe I'm too ugly for him. Too fat. Too whatever."

"Sally." I frowned at her and jumped up. I pulled her arms up and pulled her up from the bed. "Look at me," I said loudly as her eyes drifted away from mine. "You're beautiful. You're kind. You're loyal. You're the most generous person I know. You are not ugly. You are far from fat." I squeezed her hands. "My brother is a fool if he doesn't see that." I looked into her grateful brown eyes and my heart broke at the pain I saw in her gaze. "You're my best friend and my sister. And you will find the perfect man for you. Maybe that's not Cody," I said with a quick smile. "And maybe TJ's not my perfect guy, either. Maybe we need to wake up and smell the roses. Maybe our Mr. Rights are out there looking for us right now."

"So you want to blow TJ off tonight, then?" she asked me with a grin. "We can go and look for the guys who are looking for us."

"That's not such a bad idea," I said, though my heart fell at her words. I knew TJ was bad news for my heart. The more time I spent with him, the more I fell for him. His eyes had this way of piercing into my soul, and his smile was like a hammer, chipping away at the wall around my heart. Every time he smiled, a dent was made. He was becoming a part of me. When he was inside of me, I felt like we were truly one.

I had to keep reminding myself that this was an illusion. These feelings, this want, this obsession, weren't real. At the end of four weeks, I was very likely to find myself torn and broken apart. I didn't know how I would survive without him, and that scared me. We'd only just gotten into this arrangement. We'd only just begun this farce. We'd only just begun, but already I was blinded by my love for him. I walked away from Sally and grabbed my phone and punched in TJ's numbers.

"What are you doing?" Sally screeched, her eyes widening as she watched me making the call.

"Morning, sunshine." TJ's voice was silky and smooth as he picked up the phone.

"Morning," I said. "I have some bad news."

"What bad news?" His tone changed and I swallowed hard. Sally was shaking her head at me and frowning.

"Are you crazy?" she whispered. "I was joking."

"I can't come tonight," I said softly as I smiled at Sally. I needed to be a good friend more than I needed to be a good fake fiancée.

"What are you talking about?" TJ's voice was angry.

"I have to do something else tonight."

"You have a date?" His tone was deadly and I shivered. Who knew that he would get so pissed off so quickly? And why would he think I had a date?

"Um, not technically," I squeaked out.

"Not technically?" he said softly, slowly, and I waited for him to continue before speaking. "What does that mean, Mila? Do I have to remind you of our deal? Of the contract that you signed?"

"TJ, I'm just going out with Sally," I said quickly before he started getting carried away. "She's feeling down."

"Mila." Sally glared at me.

"I mean, she wanted us to go out and see if we meet the men of our dreams." I paused as I listened to the silence on the other side of the phone. Even Sally was looking at me with a shocked expression. "That came out wrong," I said in a quiet tone. "TJ?" I asked, wondering what he was thinking.

"You want to bow out of your obligation tonight so you can go and tart yourself up and meet strange men?"

"I didn't say I was going to tart myself up and I said the men of our dreams, our soul mates, not strange men."

"So you want to meet the man of your dreams tonight and then come and fuck me tomorrow night? What are you going to tell him if he asks you out? 'Sorry, I can't go because the other man I'm seeing wants to bend me over and fuck me?' "

"TJ," I gasped, aghast, but also slightly turned on.

"What?" he said and chuckled, but he didn't sound amused. "I guess that was slightly wrong. I should have said that you want me to fuck you as badly as I want to. I'm sure your panties are wet right now, aren't they?" His voice became lower and rougher. "I bet you're wishing I were with you right now so I could spank that ass and pull those panties to the side as I bend you over and slam into you from behind."

"I'm going to the mall to buy a new dress," I said stiffly as I changed the subject, embarrassed that I was feeling turned on by his words, and in front of Sally who was looking at me with a quizzical expression. "The dress is for your party tonight," I continued. "So I'll be using the credit card you gave me."

"So now you're coming?" he said in a tone that said he'd achieved exactly what he'd wanted. "I guess you're missing my big—"

"TJ!" I almost shouted as I cut him off. "You're too much." I rolled my eyes at Sally, whose eyes at narrowed at me. "Yes, I'm coming," I said stiffly. "I'll let Sally cry herself to sleep while we're out partying."

"Oh, we'll be doing a lot more than partying," he said in an amused tone, his voice deep. "Maybe tell her you'll be getting the fuck of your life. Maybe that will make her feel better about being ditched."

"You're disgusting," I said, as I felt my stomach stirring.

"You don't feel that way when I'm inside of you. You didn't feel that way when I had you up on that roof. You didn't feel that way the other morning when I was going down on you. You didn't think I was disgusting when you—"

"TJ!" I screeched.

"What?" He laughed. "Am I embarrassing you?"

I was silent as I waited for him to change the subject.

"I sure hope not," he said silkily. "I have a lot more to show you. I have plans for us, Mila."

"I know," I said softly, a small smile on my face as I rolled my eyes and shook my head at Sally. "I have plans for you as well."

"Oh?" he said, his tone curious. "What plans?"

"You'll see," I said with a small laugh. "You're not the only kinky bitch on the phone," I said, and then before he could speak, I said, "Pick me up at seven." And then I hung up the phone.

"Whoa, what was that about?" Sally said eagerly as she gazed at me. "And kinky bitch? Where did that come from?"

"I have no idea." I laughed. "I can't believe I said that." I groaned. "Kinky bitch? Oh my gosh, I can't believe I said that. He just kept saying stuff trying to turn me on, so I wanted to give him a taste of his own medicine."

"What do you have planned?" Her eyes were wide as she stared at me. "You've been holding back on me, girl."

"I have nothing planned." I groaned. "I just said that to him to make him think I had something planned."

"Oh." She giggled. "You need to think of something then."

"You think so?" I asked, groaning. "I mean, I have no idea what I can do that would make him believe that I'm a kinky bitch."

"You can do whatever you want." Sally smiled, but I could tell from the look on her face that she was doubtful.

"What am I doing, Sally?" I sighed, my head suddenly feeling heavy and my stomach wracked with nerves. "I feel like I'm playing a role, being some character I'm not and I just don't know what to do. I feel so happy being with him, but it all seems so fleeting. Like I don't know what he really wants, and if it's the kinky sex that's important to him, well, how's that supposed to make me feel?"

"I don't know what to say." She chewed on her lower lip. "I wish I knew what to say. I want to say all the things you want to hear, like this is going to grow and work out, but I don't know. I mean, this is real life, right? When do guys ever really change? I mean, do you feel like there's a possibility that he really likes you, like-likes you, likes you?"

"I used to think that," I said and then I paused. "Actually, I don't know if what I felt was real or if it was all in my head. Some sort of hope manifesting itself in me and making me see things that aren't real."

"Don't overthink it," Sally said and then grabbed my hand. "Just see what he says and does. I mean, you've waited your whole life for him, you might as well see exactly what he's open to, what he might really be feeling."

"Yeah." I nodded and smiled, but my heart sank as I thought about her words. They were exactly the same sort of words I'd said to her before about Cody, but what did they really mean? Nothing. Sally and I were both keeping hope alive, but I wasn't sure if it was worth it. Were we wasting our lives and silently killing ourselves slowly with the wait?

"So WHERE SHOULD WE GO?" I asked Sally as we got into her car. "Macy's? Dillard's?"

"Macy's?" She looked at me and laughed. "Are you out of your mind?"

"What's wrong with Macy's?" I laughed, trying to forget all my worries and just enjoy the afternoon out.

"You have a black credit card." She grinned at me. "With what I can only assume is a massive limit. Actually, do you know the limit?"

"No," I said, shaking my head. "I have no idea."

"Call the number on the back of the card." She turned the key in the ignition and started her car, but turned to me instead of pulling out of the driveway. "Come on, Mila."

"Seriously, Sally?" I shook my head. "I'm not calling to find out the limit. They aren't going to tell me anyway."

"Why not?" Her eyes crinkled as she stared at me. I knew that look in her eyes. She wanted to know and she wasn't going to back down.

"Fine." I giggled. "You know this makes us horrible people, right?"

"Why does it make us horrible? Remember when we got our first credit card in college? Remember how we called every week to see if the limit had been raised?"

"That's because we were stupid and wanted to buy things we couldn't afford." I laughed as I pulled out the card. "Thank God we only got thousand-dollar limits. You know how long it took me to pay that off?"

"I thought you were still paying it off." Sally smirked and I laughed as I hit her playfully in the shoulder.

"You're mean."

"And you're a shopaholic." She grinned. "However, at least you aren't a user. You're not going to go crazy with TJ's card."

"I would never do that," I said and dialed the credit card phone number on my cell and put it on speakerphone. I shook my head at Sally as she grinned at me, waiting eagerly to hear what the limit was.

I have to admit that I was slightly excited myself to find out what the limit would be. Not that I would come close to using all of the money. Or even using the card again after I bought this dress. I didn't want TJ to think I was taking advantage of the situation.

My heart felt sad as I thought about him and the situation we were in. I was happy that we were kind of dating, if dating was what we could call our situation. I just didn't know. We were seeing each other. We were having sex. I liked him—well, loved him. I thought he kind of liked me. However, I was also his fake fiancée, and I wasn't sure if that negated everything. Was he my boyfriend? Would he ever really be my boyfriend? I tried not to dwell on all the things in my mind. It made me doubt the relationship I found myself in.

I looked down at the phone and listened to a voice welcoming me to American Express. I punched in the numbers on the card and waited for them to ask me to verify some sort of password, so that I could look at Sally and say, "See? I can't find out that info." I was shocked when the voice asked me what I wanted to do next. I pressed 2 to hear my available balance and both Sally and I gasped loudly when the voice said, "You have an available credit limit of one hundred thousand dollars." I pressed END on the phone and looked at Sally with wide eyes. "Did I just hear that correctly?" I said, feeling slightly dazed.

"If you heard one hundred thousand dollars, then yes." She grinned at me, her eyes bright. "I cannot believe it."

"I cannot believe it, either." I put the card back in my wallet. "He's crazy."

"Yeah, he is." Sally started laughing. "Does he not know you?"

"Whatever." I giggled as we pulled out of the driveway. "I'm responsible."

"Since when?" She raised an eyebrow at me. "Last week?"

"Last week is as good as ever." I laughed. "Seriously, though, I'm not going to take advantage of the situation. It's just for this dress."

"Uh huh," Sally said. "And some new sexy bras, underwear, heels, maybe a new trench coat, a leather jacket, um—"

"A leather jacket?" I said, interrupting her. "Why would I be getting a leather jacket?"

"Because they're so cute." She giggled. "I notice you didn't ask why you should get the trench coat." She winked. "Bow chicka bow wow."

"Sally, you're so immature." I giggled. "I'm not going to go crazy on the card and I'm going to pay back whatever I spend."

"Okay." Sally didn't bat an eye, but her voice was unbelieving. "Whatever you say."

"I am." I laughed. "Though it might not be in terms of cash money."

"Like I said, bow chicka bow wow."

"Ha ha, he's lucky." I giggled. "Most guys would love to have this." I danced around in her seat, suddenly feeling light and happy. "And if anyone ever saw me or heard me saying that, they would think I was a ho."

"A ho, ho, ho." Sally nodded and looked at me. "So where shall we go, then? To the boutiques downtown?"

"I guess so." I shrugged. "You think they'll have anything there?"

"Yup." She nodded. "There's this new haute couture dress shop next to the cupcake store. I think they have vintage Chanel and Vera Wang and some Versace gowns."

"That sounds expensive." I frowned.

"Says the hundred-thousand lady." Sally laughed.

"I don't wanna be the hundred-thousand-dollar ho." I giggled.

"Who, you?" Sally said as she turned on her radio and I turned it up as it connected to the Bluetooth on her phone and the latest Pitbull song started playing. I just laughed in my seat and stared out of the window as Sally drove. I felt excited about the evening, though I wasn't sure what to expect.

"Your phone is ringing, Mila." Sally tapped me on the shoulder to break me out of my daydream.

"Oops," I said as I grabbed my phone out of my bag. "Hello," I said as I placed it next to my face quickly.

"Where are you?" TJ said softly, his voice sending a warm feeling down my spine.

"I'm in the car with Sally. We're going to get a dress and a few other necessities," I added, feeling slightly guilty.

"Good." He sounded pleased. "Tell Sally that I'd be more than happy to treat her to a new dress as well, for taking you out."

"What?" I said, surprised by his generosity, though I really shouldn't have been. "You don't have to do that."

"I want to," he said softly. "Tell her to get something nice and we can have her and Cody over this weekend, right after you move in."

"Like a double date?" I said hesitantly, not sure if that was such a good idea.

"Or just a dinner," he said smoothly. "Just four friends eating together."

"Okay," I said, disappointment swelling in my belly. *Friends.* That dreaded word that made me come back down to earth again.

"There's no need for expectations," he continued. "We can't make them get together. They aren't us."

"So are *we* together?" I asked, wanting to know exactly what we were to each other. Hope once again filled me. Maybe he really was into me after all.

"Of course we're together—you're my fiancée," he said and I wanted to interrupt him. I wanted to say that that part was a lie and ask what the real truth was between us, but I was scared that he would say that there was nothing real between us. I was scared that he would say that this was it. And I didn't want to hear that. I couldn't hear that. It would break me. And right now I wanted to believe that it was more, even if that was just a farce. I didn't want to know the truth. I didn't want my bubble to burst already. Not now. Not yet. I wasn't sure I could go through with all of my plans if I thought he didn't have any real feelings for me. If I thought that I was just a booty-call to him.

Maybe I could make him fall in love with me. Maybe if I played this role perfectly, he would suddenly realize that he didn't want this to be an act. My face felt cold as I realized how much of my heart I was putting on the line here. All of a sudden, I felt sick that I was letting myself in for a big fall and it scared the hell out of me.

"Okay, well, we're pulling up to a music store that Sally wants to go into now," I said as I looked out of the window at some trees. "I'll talk to you later."

"Send me photos of the dresses you're choosing between," he said softly. "I want to help you choose."

"You don't care." I laughed, my heart racing at the thought of him helping me choose a dress.

"I want to see them before you choose which one you're going to buy," he said softly.

"Okay," I said, though I knew that I wasn't going to be sending him any photos.

"When do you think you'll arrive at the store?" he asked again. "I have a meeting in an hour, but it won't last more than an hour."

"Oh, I'm not sure," I said honestly. "It's some place that Sally knows, but I've never been there before."

"Text me when you arrive," he said.

"Um, okay," I said. "I'd better go now. Sally is waiting on me to get out of the car."

"Okay, text me," he said and hung up the phone. I placed the phone back into my bag and looked at Sally who was glancing at me with a smile.

"What was that about, Ms. Liar?" Her eyes searched mine for a few seconds before facing the traffic again.

"Why are you calling me a liar?" I asked, my face pink as I stared in front of me.

"You're not going to send him photos of any of the dresses. And we didn't pull up to any boutique" She laughed. "He's going to be sitting there waiting and he's going to be very disappointed."

"I don't think he'll be disappointed." I laughed, but all of a sudden all I could think about was that—once again—what he wanted from me came down to something sexual.

"Sure, he will." She pulled down a one-way street and gave me a quick glance. "Men are visual creatures. He most probably can't wait to see."

"Oh well, he's in for a disappointment," I said as she pulled up to a store. "I'll text him and let him know we've arrived, but I won't be sending any pics, that way he's not waiting and wondering."

"Oh, Mila." Sally grinned at me.

"What??"

"Nothing." She shrugged. "Text him."

"I'm going to." I grabbed my phone and started punching in my message, feeling angry and not really sure why. Well, that's a lie; I knew why I was angry. I was angry that I cared so much. I was angry that the only real interest TJ seemed to show in me was in regards to sex. I was angry that I couldn't control my feelings of worry and hope that intermingled with the love I felt for him in my heart. Even though we were closer now than we'd ever been in our lives, I felt the most distant from him. I didn't feel like I was able to be myself with him because I was so scared of letting him in. I was scared that I'd fall in love with him and start to tell myself he was feeling the same way. I was scared that if I started to believe in my dreams and fairy tales, my whole world would come crashing down around me. I turned away from Sally and typed into my phone, suddenly letting my anxiety feed into anger.

Me: *I don't need your help picking a dress.*

TJ: *I didn't say you needed my help,* came the immediate reply.

Me: *Good.*

TJ: *Send me photos.*

Me: *No.*

TJ: *Stop being childish.*

Me: *Stop acting like my dad.*

TJ: *Your dad wants to see you in your underwear?*

Me: *You're disgusting.*

TJ: *That's not what you said last night.*

Me: *Grow up.*

TJ: *I thought I was acting too adult.*

Me: *Goodbye, TJ.*

TJ: *Send me nudies then.*

Me: *You wish.*

TJ: *I do. :)*

Me: *TJ!*

TJ: *Mila!*

Me: *You're insufferable.*

TJ: *You're sexy.*

Me: *Whatever.*

TJ: *I can picture your lips right now.*

Me: *Whatever.*

TJ: *I can picture my cock in your lips right now.*

Me: *TJ!*

TJ: *Yeah, that's what I'll have you screaming.*

I shook my head and tried not to smile. I wasn't feeling angry anymore. Anxious still, yes—but angry, no. I wasn't sure what it was about TJ, but he had a way of affecting my emotions without even being there. Just interacting with him made me happy. I suppose that was one of the side effects of love.

Oh how I loved and hated being in love with him. It made me feel like I was soaring through the world. Just picturing his face made me happy. And it scared me. It scared me that he had so much power over my emotions. I'd never really thought about it until recently. Until we'd become a fake couple. But now that I knew, it made me fearful. He was almost like a puppet master with my emotions.

I wasn't sure what was going to happen. I wasn't sure when the bottom was going to drop out and I was going to go flying through the vastness of an empty sky. I knew what it would feel like, though. It would feel like I was floating through the universe, by myself, empty, void of emotion and all air.

I knew the feeling because I felt it now sometimes. Late at night. When he was sleeping and gone from the conscious world. Then I would just stare at his face. I'd marvel at how handsome he was. I'd think about how I just wanted to touch his face softly, and how I wanted to run my hands through his hair. It wasn't even in a sexual way. It was just that touching him, being with him, provided me with something so innate, so filling that it was all I craved.

But I didn't touch him, because I didn't have that right. Yes, we were sleeping together. Yes, he and I were closer than we'd ever been before, but it was all superficial and sexual. It wasn't deep. It wasn't a loving, adoring relationship. It wasn't what I craved and wanted with all my heart. I wasn't able to just touch him when I wanted. I knew that. I knew that we weren't there and that's what kept me up at night. That's what made me sometimes stop suddenly, my heart growing cold, my stomach feeling fearful, and my head feeling heavy. TJ wasn't mine. He might never be mine and I didn't know if I could live with that.

"So, what did you say?" Sally interrupted my slightly depressing thoughts and I turned to her with a smile.

"I told him there is no way in hell he's getting any photos of me in any dresses. I'm not Julia Roberts and this isn't *Pretty Woman*."

"Mila." Sally laughed and linked arms with me. "You're too much, you know that?"

"Yes." I giggled. "This store looks nice. Hopefully they have something that will fit me and make me look fabulous."

"I guarantee you will look fabulous." Sally grinned as we walked into the very expensive-looking boutique.

"And sexy." I laughed.

"You always look sexy." Sally winked at me and then purred like a cat. I burst out laughing and then tried to quiet my laughter as I noticed two of the sales ladies staring at us like we were something the cat had dragged in from the alleyway. Something not entirely welcome.

"Can we help you?" A slightly older lady with perfectly coiffed blond hair approached us with a thin smile.

"We're just looking at dresses." Sally smiled back confidently and flicked her hair back. "My friend is going to an important party tonight so she wants to make sure that she has a dress worthy of the occasion."

"Oh, well, we can definitely help." The lady's eyes fell to me and I could see that she was sizing me up. "Our dresses are very expensive, ma'am." She looked at me in the eyes and I knew she was thinking that my Target and Ross bargain clothes had not impressed her. "There's a T.J. Maxx up the street." She continued as she stared at me. "It might be a bit more affordable."

"I think we'll still have a look," Sally said, her voice loud as she looked at the lady dismissively. "Thanks for your help."

"We should leave," I whispered at Sally. "She's a bitch."

"Forget her." Sally shook her head. "All the sales ladies in these places are bitches. Our goal is to get you a hot dress. We have to ignore them."

"I guess." I sighed and made a face. "I just really don't feel good about giving her money."

"If we buy a dress here, we'll ask for the owner's name and then send a scathing letter, okay?" Sally grinned at me. "That way, while she might get some commission, she'll still get in some trouble."

"Okay." I nodded. "Deal." I looked around the store and my eyes grew wide at the ample assortment of evening dresses. "I don't know how we're going to choose a dress." I made a face. "I don't even think half of these will fit me. They all look like size zero."

"Many are size zero because they are straight from the designer," Sally said, nodding in agreement. "But there will be many that aren't. And tonight, we're going to have you in a long red dress, with a plunging neckline and a high slit up the legs."

"Whoa, what?" My eyes nearly bulged out. "That sounds a bit much."

"You need to be a bit much." Sally raised an eyebrow at me. "This is TJ, remember? The love of your life. You want him to want you more than anything else in the world, don't you?"

"Yeah, but not just for sex. I want him to want me for my mind *and* my body. I want him to think he can't live without me."

"This is step one," Sally said. "Guys think with their small heads first. You need him to be obsessing over you and wanting you in his bed at all times. Then he'll start to realize just how much you mean to him in every area of his life."

"I guess," I sighed. "I just don't know if TJ will ever feel that way about me. He's not the guy I thought he was, you know? He seems more damaged than I thought. A bit darker and deeper, not just the joker I always thought."

"He's dark because he's into kinky sex, Mila." She laughed, but I shook my head at her as our eyes caught.

"No, it's more than that. I don't know how to explain it, but it's more than that." I sighed. "But who knows? Maybe I'm imagining it. Maybe it's not anything other than what I want to think and believe." I paused as I heard my phone beeping. I looked down and saw TJ's name on the screen and ignored it. I didn't need his playful teasing right now. Not when I was already so confused about everything.

"Stop overthinking everything, Mila." Sally gave me a pointed look. "I know you over-analyze everything and sometimes that is good, but this is not one of those situations. Just let it go where it goes."

"I guess so. That's hard, though."

"I know." She nodded. "But life is hard. No one ever said it was going to be easy."

"I want it to be easy." I moaned. "I want him to just wake up and say, Mila, I love you, let's make this real."

"Maybe he will," Sally said softly, her eyes on mine. "And maybe he won't. But don't live out your days waiting for that. Enjoy whatever you have now. It's good now, or at least good enough, right?"

"Yeah," I said softly. "It's good enough. It's more than I thought I would have with him."

"Then enjoy." Sally walked away from me then and up to a dress rack. "Now stop thinking and start looking. We need to get you a dress that's going to blow TJ away."

"Yeah, that would be nice," I agreed and walked over to a display next to her and started thumbing through the dresses, though I wasn't really seeing them. All I was thinking about was the look I hoped to see on TJ's face when he saw me. I wanted his eyes to widen. I wanted him to look impressed, taken aback. I wanted his eyes to rove all over my body and not want to look away. I wanted him to want me more than he'd ever wanted anyone in the world. I wanted him to look at me as if I were the last person in the world. I wanted him to think I was the most beautiful woman he'd ever seen. Not that I was or would ever be. There were far more beautiful women out there, but I wanted TJ to look at me as if I were one of them.

I wanted time to stand still. I got shivers just thinking about it. And then I started to feel teary-eyed again because I knew it would never happen. TJ would never look at me as if I were that special someone. I couldn't imagine it. As much as I wanted it, I just couldn't see it happening.

"Ooh, what about this?" Sally held up a dress to show me. It was short, black and the top was made of some sort of transparent lace.

"Sally, people will see my bra or my breasts." I shook my head. "I don't want them seeing either."

"Fine." She grinned and put it back on the rack. "Though, it's a fucking sexy dress."

"That it is." I laughed and continued looking through the dresses. My hand stopped on a long cream dress with pearls running along the neckline. "What about this?" I asked Sally and held the dress up.

"Are you a grandma going to prom?" Sally made a face. "No way, that's not sexy at all."

"Fine." I laughed and kept thumbing through the dresses. My hand stopped on a delicate, sexy black dress with a lace back and a long slit. "What about this?" I said breathlessly as I held it up for her to see.

"Wow." Sally's eyes widened as she glanced at the dress in my hand. "That's hot."

"You don't think it's too much?"

"Is there such a thing as too much?"

"Yes," I laughed. "There is definitely such a thing as too much. I don't want to be the skank at the party."

"You, my dear, could never be a skank."

"Yes, I could." I laughed and then looked at the dress again. "But

I'm still going to try it on." I smiled at her. "Maybe it will go right up to the ho line but not pass it."

"That's a fine line." Sally laughed and we grinned at each other, both of our worries forgotten in that moment as we shopped.

"Thanks for coming with me, Sally. It really means a lot to me."

"Shh." She rolled her eyes and pushed me. "Don't get emotional. Just go and change and let me see how hot you look."

"Fine." I grinned and looked around for a dressing room. "I hope it looks good," I said as I walked towards the back of the store.

"It will look great, and if it doesn't, there are plenty more dresses to try on."

"I know," I said, though I knew I would feel disappointed if the dress in my hands didn't look good. I'd only seen it for a few seconds, but I was already drawn to it. It was intricate and pretty and I loved the look of it. I just hoped that it would look good on me.

I walked into the dressing room and pulled the curtain, hanging the dress on a hanger carefully before setting my bag down. I started to take off my clothes slowly, staring at myself in the mirror as I did so. I paused for a few seconds and just stared at my face up close. I wasn't sure what it was about dressing room mirrors, but they always seemed so much clearer than my mirrors at home. I suppose it had to do with the lighting in the dressing room.

I stared into my brown eyes and then at my lashes, still slightly tinged with black mascara that I hadn't gotten off. I had some small lines around my eyes and slightly darker bags. I wrinkled my nose as I stared at the lines and tried not to sigh. I stared at my cheeks, seeing that my skin looked smooth, except for a few freckles, and I smiled at myself and then rolled my eyes at how idiotic I was to be smiling at myself in a dressing-room mirror.

I pulled my top off and my jeans down and studied my body. My bra looked old and funky, though I was happy with the fact that my boobs looked luscious. I then looked at my stomach and grimaced.

There was definitely no six-pack there or even a faint glimmering of abs. I needed to work on that. TJ had such a perfect body and I wanted to be able to match that. Maybe that would make him want me more. My eyes fell farther, to my thighs and calves, and I turned to the side to check out my ass. It was still pretty flat, but was a bit more pert than usual, thanks to all my squats. Overall, I was pleased with what I saw, if not ecstatic. I shook my head at myself and then reached over to grab the dress off of the hanger, when I suddenly froze. I'd heard a deep, familiar-sounding voice, and my body started shaking. It couldn't be, could it?

"Mila?" TJ's deep voice echoed through the store and my face grew heated. How was TJ here?

"TJ, what are you doing here?" Sally asked, surprised. I'm sure she was wondering how he was here as well.

"Where's Mila?" TJ sounded annoyed.

"She's in the changing room," Sally said, her voice stiff. "What are you doing here?"

"I told Mila I wanted to see the dresses."

"I thought she told you no."

"So?" he said in an amused tone, his voice coming closer. "Mila, you there?"

I opened my mouth, but no words would come out. I was in shock.

"Mila?" His voice came closer.

"TJ?" I squeaked out finally. "What are you doing here?"

"I texted you and you didn't respond," he said accusingly from right outside my room.

"I was busy," I said defensively.

"I figured."

"How did you know where I was?"

"What?" TJ said slowly.

"How did you know where I was? I didn't tell you."

37

"I shared your location."

"What?" I frowned, not understanding him. "What does that mean?"

"I went into your phone and shared your location with my number," he said matter-of-factly, as if there were nothing wrong with that. "I wanted to make sure I could—"

"SPY ON ME?" I shouted, interrupting him. "How dare you?"

"I just wanted to make sure you were safe and that I could find you if anything happened." He sounded sheepish now.

"If what happened, TJ?" I was annoyed.

"I don't know."

"Did you share your location with me as well?" I asked softly, though I already knew the answer.

"I didn't think about it," he said after a few seconds. "Sorry, I should have done that as well."

"Yeah, sure, that's the reason why I'm upset. Not. TJ, you can't just go into my phone and share my location without even asking me."

"I'm sorry," he said, his tone unreadable. I wasn't sure if he was really sorry or if he was just saying that.

"Sure you are." I shook my head from inside my dressing room. "Anyway, what can I do for you, TJ?"

"I came to see your dress choices."

"I told you that I didn't want to show them to you."

"I thought that was just via text. I thought, in person, you'd be happy to show me."

"TJ, don't you have work to do?"

"I always have work to do, but I wanted to make time to see you," he said softly. "I've been thinking about you all day. I thought it would be romantic of me to come down and see you during the day. Don't you girls like romantic gestures?"

"I guess." I bit down on my lower lip. What did that mean? Why was he trying to be romantic? Was he falling for me, after all?

"So can I see you in at least one dress?"

"Fine," I sighed. "Hold on, I'm putting one on right now."

"I'm waiting," he said, his tone lighter now—happy, even. I was itching to see his face and his smile, but I wasn't about to open the curtain while I was still in my underwear.

"Hold on," I said as I slipped the dress over my head and sucked my breath in to pull it down. I paused as I pressed my breasts in with one hand and continued to pull the dress down. I was praying to God that the material wouldn't rip. That would be all that I needed.

"Mila?" TJ sounded impatient.

"TJ," I said, annoyed, as I sucked in my stomach so that the material could go down. When it got to my hips, I paused, as I wasn't sure if I could get it all the way down. I shimmied back and forth and then stood still, pulling the material down my legs. Then I looked in the mirror and started grinning at my reflection. The dress looked amazing and, even though it was tight, it held me in in all the right places and made my body look a lot tighter and fitter than it was. I just stared at my reflection for a few seconds before a feeling of shyness overwhelmed me. What if TJ didn't like it? What if he didn't think I looked amazing? What if—?

"Mila, is it on yet?" TJ said, his voice lower. In response, I opened the curtain and gave him a small glare to show him that I was angry at his impatience. "Ooh," he said as he stared at me, his eyes widening and a slow grin spreading over his face before he gave a loud whistle. "Worth the wait." He grinned, his eyes travelling down my body and stopping at the long slit that went up the legs. "Definitely worth the wait."

"Let me see you, Mila." Sally hurried over and her eyes also widened as she glanced at me. "Wow, you're hot."

"Yes, she is," TJ said in response as I just stood there, grinning like a fool, feeling more flattered than I'd ever felt in my life.

"Now, you just need to get some heels," Sally said with a grin. "Some new heels to match the dress."

"I have heels." I shook my head at Sally. I wasn't going to go crazy with TJ's credit card.

"Not that match that dress," Sally said and grabbed my hand. "Turn around," She said as she spun me in a circle. "Wow, the back is gorgeous as well," Sally said and she nodded at me as I faced her again. "Great pick."

"The dress is amazing," TJ said softly, his eyes searching mine for a few seconds as I looked at him. "Almost as amazing as you."

"Thank you," I said, my heart racing at his words. What did they mean? Was he really falling for me?

"I'm proud to call you my fake fiancée," he said, his eyes moving away. "I couldn't have picked anyone better for the role."

"Thanks," I said, my smile falling slightly. Was he answering my unasked question? Was he putting me in my place in case I got any other ideas?

"You look really gorgeous, Mila. Simply beautiful," he said, looking back at me, his expression slightly bewildered. "I should go," he said and took a step back.

"Go?" I asked, looking at him in confusion. "You just got here." I laughed at him, feeling slightly uncomfortable.

"And I see you're in good hands." He looked at Sally and then back at me, before taking a quick step towards me. He gave me a kiss on the cheek and then just stared into my eyes for a few seconds before giving me the most beguiling smile. "I'm going to go back to work now."

"Okay," I said, feeling breathless as I smiled back at him. "I'll see you tonight?"

"I'll pick you up at seven," he said, his eyes becoming closed off again. "Don't eat."

"Okay," I said again and just nodded and watched him as he

walked out of the store. Then I turned to Sally. "I'm not sure what just happened there." I looked at her with wide, confused eyes.

"He likes you." She smiled at me, but I could see that she looked dazed as well. "He's a crazy, psycho stalker, but I think he might have real feelings for you."

"You think so?"

"Yeah." She nodded and then reached over and grabbed my hand. "Though, I don't know what that means. I don't know if he even knows. I don't know if he realizes. And I don't know if he wants to be that guy."

"What guy?" I frowned at her, not really understanding.

"The forever guy," she said slowly. "I don't know if he's comfortable with his emotions."

"What do you mean?" I said, my voice rising.

"I don't know." She shook her head and shrugged. "Ignore me. Let's get you out of this dress so you can buy it, then we can go and get you some new heels."

"Sally." I laughed at her insistence that I get new shoes as well. "This dress is enough. I don't want him to think I'm taking advantage of him."

"Oh, I don't think he'll think that," she said and turned around. "If anything, he's taking advantage of you," she said as she walked away. I walked back into the dressing room; heart racing as I ignored her whispered words. I didn't want to think about anything too deeply. I didn't really understand what was going on between TJ and me, and at this point, I didn't want to.

"I'LL HAVE THIS DRESS, PLEASE." I walked up to the sales lady who was now looking at me with a certain admiration in her eyes. I was positive it was because she'd seen TJ and was most probably wondering how someone like me had landed a stud like him.

"Certainly, madam. Anything else?" She beamed at me and I tried not to roll my eyes.

"Nope. I would've bought some other dresses for the balls I'm going to next month, but I think I'll go elsewhere," I said as I pulled out my new black card and dropped it on the counter. "Thanks, though."

She picked up the card, her eyes slightly cold as she looked at me. "Can I see some ID, madam?"

"Of course." I stared at her sweetly as I took out my driver's license. It took everything in me not to gloat at her and tell her *I told you I could afford a dress in here, biatch.* Though, of course, I didn't. Not only because it would have been childish, but also because it wasn't really true. I couldn't afford crap in here, but I wasn't going to tell her that.

"So who was that young man that just came in?" she asked me casually and I could see that the other sales lady was paying attention now as well.

"My fiancé." I grinned nonchalantly.

"Oh." Her lips thinned as she glanced at me again and I just smiled widely at her. In that moment, I felt like a million dollars and I was going to remind myself to never judge a book by its cover in the future as well.

Chapter Three

Mila

MY FEET WERE STARTING TO hurt in my heels. I'd known that four-inch-heels were too high to be comfortable, but Sally had talked me into buying them because they made my calves look "killer." I was now regretting following my vanity—especially seeing as TJ had barely glanced at me or talked to me since we'd arrived at the party. And even though other men were giving me appreciative looks, it didn't really matter to me.

The only one I wanted thinking I looked hot was TJ. And boy, did he look hot tonight with his crisp white shirt and black tuxedo. His short black hair was slicked back and his green eyes were illuminated on his tan face. His shoulders were strong and muscular and I couldn't stop myself from staring at his shapely, muscular legs and strong butt as he walked. I'd never experienced such lust from just looking at a man before, but TJ was driving me crazy. Maybe it was because I knew exactly what his strong, athletic body could do to me and I was missing the attention. He could at least give me some sort of sexy "I want to fuck you right now" smile. But no, nothing. I sipped on my wine and tried to stifle a sigh. I had issues. I didn't want our relationship to be all about sex, but all I could think about right now was being with TJ in a strictly carnal way. The hairs on my neck started to stand on end and I looked to the right to see that TJ was staring at me with narrowed eyes.

"What?" I asked after almost a minute of him just staring at me.

"What?" he asked and blinked, his eyes not leaving mine but a smile not reaching his face either.

"Nothing," I said and looked away, feeling flushed and hot. Why was he just staring at me and not saying anything? My stomach churned as I thought about the look that had been in his eyes. What did it mean? I was going to drive myself crazy by over-analyzing every look he gave me.

"See that door over there?" TJ moved closer to me, so that his body was right next to mine. I could feel his body heat right next to me, even though we weren't touching. I looked over at him and he nodded to a door on the other side of the room.

"Yeah." I nodded. "Why?"

"I want you to go into that room and wait for me."

"Why?" I looked up and stared into his eyes.

"You'll see. I want it to be a surprise." He winked at me and his hand slid down to my ass.

"TJ, there are people standing right outside that door." My eyes widened as his hand rested on the small of my back. "I'm not going in there to wait for you to do whatever you want to do to me." Though, I desperately wanted to just run to the room so that I could wait for him to take me.

"You know what I want to do to you." He leaned down and kissed my cheek and moved his mouth to my ear, his tongue licking me lightly before he whispered, "I want to pull that sexy, slinky dress off of you, but I won't. Instead I'll just pull it up as high as it can go. Then I'll reach down and I'll move your panties to the side. Actually, no, maybe I'll just rip them off, keep them in my pocket as a party souvenir." His voice was husky and I shivered at his words. "Then I'll bend you over so your ass is in the air and I'll touch you lightly, delicately, and caress you before I give you what we both want."

"I think you'll find that to be a difficult task," I said softly, batting my eyelashes up at him, though I was finding it hard to talk because I was so turned on. My body was on fire and I found myself wanting to play along with him and his sexy talk. I wanted to show him that I wasn't scared of his sexual side. In fact I craved it. It turned me on. Even though I loved him and was scared that this was all about sex for him, I wanted him to know that I could give as good as I got.

"Why is that?" He leaned back and his eyes bore into mine intensely as if we were the only two people in the room.

"Because I don't have any panties on," I said, leaning over and whispering in his ear before smiling sweetly. I heard his sharp intake of breath and then walked away from him quickly and headed over to talk to a small group of women who were standing next to us. "Hi, I'm Mila," I said as I approached the group. They looked towards me curiously, with surprised expressions. "I'm TJ Walker's fiancée," I said, feeling slightly out of place like some sort of intruder.

"We know who you are," the oldest-looking lady answered with a tight smile. "Glad you could join us tonight."

"Oh, it's my pleas—"

"Excuse us, ladies." TJ grabbed my arm as he interrupted me and pulled me away from the circle of women. "I need to talk to my fiancée."

"TJ," I gasped as he pulled me. "What are you doing? People are looking."

"They can look. They can listen. I don't care," he said as we headed towards the door. "I have an investigation to take care of."

"What investigation?" I asked, confused, my heart thudding.

"I want to know if, one, you really have no underwear on and, two, if you are as wet as I think you are right now?"

"TJ Walker," I squeaked as we made our way past his father and the group of board of directors. "No way."

"Oh, I think way." He stopped abruptly and I crashed into him. His hands reached out to steady me and he held me close to his side.

He looked down into my face and smiled a sweet yet devious smile as his fingers caressed my lips. "If I haven't told you yet, that dress is very sexy," he said smoothly and his eyes fell to my partially exposed chest. "Very, very sexy."

"You've told me," I said as I gazed back at him in his black tuxedo. He looked disturbingly handsome, with his dark silky hair that was slightly too long and wild, his green eyes that glittered into mine like emeralds, haughty and superior, and his pink luscious lips that were turned up and waiting to do all sorts of naughty things to me. I bit down on his finger as it invaded my mouth and he pulled it back quickly with a look of surprise on his face.

"Feisty tonight," he said huskily. "I like it."

"You'll be liking it in the privacy of our bedroom, though, not here," I told him smartly, licking the taste of him off of my lips.

"Yes, I'll be enjoying it there as well." He grinned as he leaned closer to me. He bent down and kissed my lips and then pulled away slightly. "And I'll be enjoying it here as well."

"No, you won't," I said, grinning back at him as I leaned forward and kissed him. "Sorry about your luck, TJ."

"Oh, don't be sorry," he said, his teeth grabbing onto my lower lip so he could suck it. "My luck is quite fine."

"TJ." I grabbed onto his shoulders and pushed him back. "We can't do this here."

"I think we can," he said, but he let go of my lips and rubbed his own with his fingers. He grabbed my hands and winked. "Now, come with me."

"TJ, no, this is not an appropriate venue." I squeezed his hands and hissed. "We're not going—"

"I know about Operation Condor," he said lightly and looked back at me, his eyes looking amused as he stared at me.

"Oh, my gosh." My heart stopped for a second as I stood there, feeling embarrassed as he brought up the code name for the "seduce

TJ" plan I'd invented with Sally when I was younger. "How do you know?"

"I think you'd better come with me and find out," he said and turned back around and starting walking again. I followed alongside him, my entire body feeling hot like I was lying on a beach in the Caribbean; only I wasn't in a relaxed state. TJ stopped outside the door, turned to look at me and then grinned. "Go outside and meet me by my car," he said softly and I frowned.

"What?" I looked at him and then the door behind him. "I thought we were going in there?"

"I changed my mind." He shrugged. "We're not going in there any more."

"TJ? What's going on?" I asked him, feeling confused.

"You're about to find out." He licked his lips, grabbed my hand and before I knew what was happening, he'd pulled me behind the door into what appeared to be a bathroom.

"TJ?" I gasped as I felt his fingers sliding up under my dress.

"Just checking," he growled as his fingers found my wetness. "I just wanted to make sure I was right."

"TJ," I moaned as his fingers slid back and forth and then stopped to rub on my throbbing bud. "TJ, we can't do this here." I moaned as he slipped a finger inside of me.

"We're not going to do it here," he said huskily.

"Oh?" I looked at him in confusion, lust having taken over my faculties. "Are we going home already?"

"We're not going home," he said and shook his head, his teeth grinning at me. "Go and wait by the car for me."

"I don't understand."

"You will." He laughed. "Now go."

"Okay," I said, feeling dazed as I straightened my dress out and walked away from him back towards the door.

"That dress really does look sexy on you." He growled from behind me and pulled me back into his arms so that he could nuzzle my neck. "And those heels as well. Worth every penny I spent."

I stiffened in his arms as he mentioned the fact that he'd paid for the dress and shoes. It still made me feel slightly uncomfortable. Like I was some sort of paid woman or something.

"I like to spoil you, Mila," he whispered into my ear. "I want to spoil you. Please let me do that without you freezing up."

"Fine," I whispered as I turned my head to look at him. He gave me a quick kiss on the side of the face and then let me go.

"See you outside," he said as he lightly tapped my bottom.

"I'll be waiting," I said sassily back to him and then left the room.

I STOOD BY TJ'S CAR, wondering what the plan was. I was excited and slightly embarrassed at how exhilarated I felt while waiting in eager anticipation. I hadn't known that sex would make me feel like this. I hadn't known that the pull of the body could be even more intense than the pull of the heart. It made me start to understand why so many people slept around, but it did make me wonder if it was as intense and good if there wasn't also love. I thought back to the guys I'd dated in high school and college and wondered if I would have felt the same way about them. I doubted it. I never had super intense feelings for them and I couldn't imagine that they were as skilled as TJ.

TJ made lovemaking exciting, even slightly dangerous. I knew that he was most probably a more intense, slightly psychotic lover than most, but that made him even more intoxicating to me. Nothing about TJ was routine. Nothing about him was normal. And I loved that about him. I loved getting to know his hidden layers. It made me feel like I was getting to know him better.

"What are you thinking about?" TJ's voice was caressing as he walked towards me with a confident strut and a sly smile on his face.

"I was thinking about my ex-boyfriends," I said honestly, watching as he frowned.

"What?" He looked annoyed as he stopped in front of me.

"I was just wondering what it would have been like if we'd had sex," I said sheepishly. "If they would have wowed me in bed like you have."

TJ just stared at me then. I don't think he got the compliment I'd given him, based on the angry look on his face. My stomach sank as I realized I'd said the wrong thing.

"I mean, not that I want them to come and wow me in bed now . . . " My voice trailed off and he continued to just stare at me. "I was just thinking about the past." I made a face at him. "Say something."

"What do you want me to say?" TJ growled at me. "I think I'd rather show you than tell you."

"Show me what?"

"How I'm thinking and feeling." His eyes glittered at me. "I'll make you forget all those exes once and for all."

"It's not like I want to be with them." I sighed. "I was just telling you what was going through my mind the moment you came up to me."

"Mila," he said with a shake of his head, "enough."

"Enough what?" I gawked at him. "I haven't even really said anything. It's not like we were in bed and I screamed out one of their names or had fantasies of you being one of them."

"Mila." He came closer to me and his nostrils were flaring. "You are completely ridiculous."

"What's that supposed to mean?" I frowned at him. "I'm not ridiculous."

"If I weren't a gentleman, I would bend you over right here and now and show you what's what," TJ said, his voice throaty as he leaned down to look into my eyes.

"Yeah, I guess if you weren't a gentleman, you would do that," I said, my breath coming quickly as I looked up into his eyes, my lips a mere inch from him.

"Are you doubting the fact that I'm a gentleman?" he said, his lips moving against mine but not kissing me.

"Would that be a surprise?" I said as my lips touched his gently.

"No." He chuckled and pressed his lips against mine harder, this time actually kissing me.

"You know you're a dirty rotten scoundrel inside." I kissed him back and then tugged on his lower lip with my teeth.

"And you love it," he said, his eyes staring into mine as his hands crept around my waist. "You want me to be a dirty bastard," he said, pushing himself into me. I could feel his hardness against my lower belly and I felt a stirring inside my soul.

"I don't want you to be anything you don't want to be," I said, swallowing hard as he pulled me closer towards him.

"Aren't you considerate?" He almost purred as his hands crept up and cupped my breasts.

"Yes." I smiled innocently back at him and reached down and grabbed his package. "I'm very considerate." I squeezed gently and he groaned as he grew in my hands.

"Yes, you are." He groaned and moved his mouth to my ear and blew sensually. "I want to fuck you, Mila. I want to bend you over my car and take you from behind. It won't be romantic and it won't be slow."

"Okay," I squeaked out as I blushed.

"Are you okay with that?" He leaned back and looked at me. "Or will you consider me an asshole?"

"I don't think you're an asshole."

"I just want to make sure. I remember in your Operation Condor handbook, you had something about sex in a car. I wasn't sure if sex *over* a car was the same."

"Oh, my God." My face grew redder. "That's how you knew? You saw my notebook?"

"Maybe." He laughed and then nodded. "I read it once." He grinned. "I was waiting to see if you were ever going to make a move on me in the back seat of a car. I was disappointed that you never did."

"Oh, my God, I could die," I squealed as I desperately tried to remember exactly what I'd written in the notebook. I know I had several seduction techniques in there that I'd never used, but I couldn't remember what else I might have written about.

"It's not that bad." He laughed and then winked. "Now I can help you live out some of your fantasies."

"Those weren't my fantasies," I protested as I continued to squeeze his hardness.

"What were they, then? He grunted and thrust himself into my hands.

"They were what I thought would be your fantasies," I admitted, slightly embarrassed.

"You wanted to make my fantasies come true?"

"Yes." I nodded and cried out as he spun me around and pushed me over the hood of his car. "TJ?"

"Shh, we're making one of my fantasies come true," he said and I felt him sliding his zipper down behind me, before pulling my dress up and to the side.

"TJ?" I gasped as I felt the cool air hit my behind. "Should we be doing this here? What if someone sees us?"

"That's why we have to be quick." He grunted and I felt him thrust inside of me deep and hard.

"Ooh," I cried out as he filled me up. I fell forward and I moaned as he thrust in and out of me quickly. The car metal was cold against my collarbone, but TJ was warming me up from inside.

"Oh, Mila, you're so wet for me. You were so wet and ready for this, weren't you?"

"TJ." I moaned out his name, unable to say anything else as I felt an orgasm building up. I couldn't believe I was letting him fuck me in the parking lot, where anyone could see us, but that was part of being with TJ—the excitement, the danger, it was all an added plus. He lived life on the edge, every single day, and I was starting to enjoy that as well.

"Mila." He grabbed my hips and slammed into me, over and over again, so that I could barely breathe. His cock felt so deep inside of me that I thought I was going to pass out from the pleasure. "I'm going to come." He groaned and I allowed myself to let go completely in the last few thrusts. He collapsed on top of me after we came, and we just lay there on the car for a few seconds before he stepped back, pulled me up and straightened my dress back down.

"I want you to move in with me tomorrow," TJ said as he held me close to him. "I need to have you around all the time."

"I know, you already said that before." I panted, not wanting to think too much into it, as my body was still riding high on my orgasm. I didn't want to grow hope that he wanted me close because he was falling for me. "But I can't move in tomorrow. I still need to pack and get my stuff together."

"The day after?" He frowned.

"A few days." I laughed and touched the side of his face lightly as he pouted. "I'll move in, in a few days."

"Good," he said and then kissed me on the forehead. "That's settled then."

"Then you can have your wicked way with me whenever you want," I said teasingly, though I wasn't really joking.

"Yup." He winked and leaned over and bit down on my lip. "Whenever I want," he said as he looked into my eyes. "Just as long as you're willing."

I'm always willing crossed my mind, but instead I stayed silent and just smiled at him. Confusion and lust were invading my mind and I was starting to get caught up in the fog of emotions that TJ had always brought to my life.

"Let's go back inside." He smiled and held my hand and we walked back into the party with huge grins on our faces.

Chapter Four

TJ

One Year Ago

"I NEED YOU TO GO to Paris tomorrow, sign the contract for the Hatcher deal." My dad looked up at me, a small frown on his face. "And see if you can get them to include the patents from their glamour manufacturers."

"Tomorrow?" I frowned at him. "I can't go tomorrow."

"You have to fly out tomorrow, so you can sign the contract the following day."

"I can't go tomorrow." I shook my head, not wanting to tell him why.

"TJ, this isn't a discussion. You're going tomorrow." My dad was looking at me with narrowed eyes.

"I have something to do on Friday," I said. "You'll have to go."

I watched as my dad pursed his lips. He didn't like being disobeyed.

"Why can't you go?" he asked me, his lips thin.

"Mila's graduating," I said, noticing the dismissive look on his face.

"From high school?" He sneered.

"College," I said my voice tinged with anger. "She asked me to come watch her walk."

"Is that really important?" He stared at me, his eyes cold.

"It's important to Mila."

"Her family is going, yes?" He sighed. "Why do they need you to go? You can still give her a graduation present if you don't go."

"She asked me to go," I said, starting to get angry. "I'm not flying to Paris."

"Travis James Walker, a graduation is not more important than a fifty-million-dollar deal."

"It is to me," I said, trying to explain to him and myself why it was so important to me that I attend. "She's my best friend's sister. She's been in my life for years. This is important to her. It's important to me. I'm going."

"So you're going because you feel like it's your sister that's graduating?" My dad sneered. "Are you telling me that you wish I'd given you siblings?"

"I'm not saying anything like that," I said, my fists clenching. He didn't understand that I had deep feelings for the whole Brookstone family. He didn't understand that I considered them to be closer family than he was. He didn't understand that Mila was special and when she'd called me months ago telling me she was graduating and asked if I'd come to the ceremony, something in me had lit up. I wasn't going to miss it if I could help it.

"Fine." My dad pursed his lips. "I'm not happy and this shows me that I don't think you're anywhere near to being able to take over the company. I'm going to have to do some serious thinking."

"May I go now?" I asked, not interested in my dad's emotional and mental blackmail. If he wanted to pass on his company to someone else, he could do so.

"Yes," he said, and as I walked out of his office, I could feel his eyes boring into my back. I opened the door, closed it and continued on out of the building. I was done for the day. My heart was racing and I wasn't quite sure why I'd refused my dad on such an important deal for a college graduation. I was pretty sure that Mila wouldn't care that much if I'd missed it. But I wanted to be there. I wanted to be a part of her special occasion. I wanted to hug her and congratu-late her on finally becoming a full-grown adult. I wanted to welcome her to the world. A world she didn't know yet. I wanted to be there for her. In more ways than one.

Current Day

"Soooo . . ." Mila looked at me awkwardly, her three large suitcases set in front of her waiting to be carried to my bedroom. I had to admit that I was slightly taken aback at how much stuff she'd brought with her. I'd been expecting a duffel bag of clothes or something, not what appeared to be her entire wardrobe. I wondered what the taxi driver must have thought when he'd dropped her off. If he was anything like me, he probably thought that she was thinking that she was moving in forever. I tried not to panic at the thought, though a part of me kind of liked the idea that she'd be here with me forever.

"So?" I said with a small smile. I wasn't going to make this easy for her.

"Where should I put my suitcases?"

"Where do you want them to go?"

"In my room." She shrugged, her face turning red. I thought it was cute that she could still be embarrassed in front of me, after everything we'd done together.

"You mean our room?" I asked softly as I walked towards her. "The room with the whips and chains?"

"I guess so." She licked her lips nervously, her eyes widening slightly at my words. I knew she was wondering if I was joking or not. Actually, I take that back. I knew that she knew that I wasn't joking.

"Do you want to see my secret dungeon?" I touched her shoulder lightly and gazed into her warm brown eyes, a secret thrill running through me as I saw the curiosity in her eyes.

"Would it be a secret if I saw it?" she replied smartly and I laughed. She was still my snappy Mila, no matter what we'd done together. I'd been slightly worried that she'd be a little overwhelmed and scared of me. I did have a voracious sexual appetite and I knew that some women didn't enjoy the risks and adventures I liked to take. It made me appreciate the woman she'd grown into even more.

"Well, you'll see it eventually." I winked. "But I suppose that will be when you're naked and begging me to—"

"Ha." She rolled her eyes as she interrupted me. "I won't be begging you to do anything."

"Oh how foolish and young you are." I laughed, my fingers running along her trembling lips. "How many times do you have to be reminded otherwise?"

"Reminded of what?"

"Reminded of how good it feels to beg me. And how good it feels when I give in to your pleas."

"I don't beg and plea and you don't give in. It's not giving in if you want it as well, TJ."

"Shall I tell you what I want right now?" I said, leaning down and kissing her lips softly. She kissed me back, her tongue licking my lips before she gently sucked on my lower lip and bit down with her small, sharp teeth. I felt a stirring in my loins as my hands moved down to her waist, pulling her closer to me, so that she could feel what she was doing to me. I felt her sharp intake of breath as my hardness pressed against her stomach and I deepened our kiss, my hands falling to her ass.

"TJ," she moaned, her hands pushing me back.

"Yes," I groaned, not wanting to stop.

"My room?" she asked sweetly, batting her eyelashes up at me. "I've got some unpacking to do."

"I don't know why you brought all these clothes with you," I said as I picked up two of her suitcases. I grunted at how heavy they were. What exactly had she packed? "It's not like you're going to be wearing clothes much."

"Oh?" She tossed her long blond hair to the side and gave me a cute little smile, her nose crinkling as she gazed at me. "Is that what you think?"

"That's what I know," I growled as she poked me in the chest with her index finger. I noticed that she'd recently painted her nails a hot-pink color and I wondered if she had painted her toenails the same color as well.

"Keep fooling yourself, Mila." I laughed as I walked towards my bedroom and she followed behind. It felt strangely exciting to be welcoming Mila to my home. I'd never lived with a woman before and I wasn't sure what to expect. I know what I was hoping to expect, but I didn't want to get my hopes up.

"I brought some sheets with me, if you don't mind," she said softly as we walked into the bedroom. "I thought they would soften up the room." She gave me an impish smile as I put her cases down and turned to her. "Seeing as I live here now as well." She walked over to the bed and pulled the duvet off and handed it to me. "I might as well change the sheets now, seeing as I have you here with me."

I stood there in silence as she proceeded to pull the dark gray sheets off of my bed. To say I felt stunned was an understatement. This was all of a sudden seeming real. Realer than I'd expected. And my worry grew. What if Mila's expectations were different from mine? What if we weren't on the same page that I thought we were on? My heart skipped a beat as I stared at the back of her body while she hummed to herself happily. I was lying to myself and to her. I knew that her expectations were different. I knew that I was playing with fire. I knew that one or both of us was going to get burned, but I didn't care. I didn't care because in that moment all I could think about were my needs. And her needs. And to hell with the rest. To hell with the secrets and lies. To hell with feelings. To hell with all of it. I was going to show Mila that all the things she thought I'd been joking about were real. I was going to show her my secret dungeon. The dungeon she didn't believe was real. And I was going to have her begging me. Begging me to give her more pleasure than she'd ever known in her life. And then I was going to make her wait. And while the wait would almost kill both of us, it would only make things so much better. And then, then she would know that her dreams and fantasies about who I was and who we were together were just that— figments of her imagination. And when she realized that, I knew that life as I knew it would be over.

"TJ, don't freak out." She turned away from changing the sheets and looked at me, her expression one I didn't truly understand. "I'm not looking to change who you are, just your sheets," she said, eyes gazing into mine knowingly. Though, I wasn't sure exactly what she thought she knew.

"I'm not freaking out," I said, though that was only partially true.

"Seven, ten, twenty," she said softly and I froze as I gazed at her in shock. "That's the combination to your secret room."

"How did you know that?" I swallowed hard as I took a step towards her, the shock evident in my voice and on my face. "How did you know?" I asked again as I stepped in front of her.

"You're not the only one with secrets, TJ." She looked up at me with clear eyes, a small smile on her face. "You might realize one day that you can't underestimate me. Anywho, you found out about Operation Condor. I found out about the code."

"You might realize one day that I never did underestimate you," I said and she looked away then, something in her eyes changing, making me think that she had something to hide.

"So do I get a closet?" She changed the subject, and as much as I wanted to stop her and tell her that I would like to go back to how she knew the combination number, I didn't.

"A closet?" I grinned at her. "You want a whole closet?"

"Well, I guess a drawer could do." She rolled her eyes at me. "And I'll just live out of my suitcases for the next four weeks."

"What did you bring with you?" I asked her, wondering what on earth she had thought to pack for four weeks.

"Clothes, toiletries, books, my laptop, makeup, bubble bath—"

"Bubble bath?" I interrupted her, surprised. "You know I have bubble bath, right? Or that I can buy more if I run out."

"I like the bubble bath I buy. It's a cantaloupe melon scent and it leaves the skin really soft."

"Okay, so that's definitely for you, then." I laughed. "I don't want to smell of melon."

"It's amazing." She pouted. "Don't knock it until you try it."

"That's fine. I'll just smell you."

"That sounds so creepy." She giggled and I watched as she pulled out two throw pillows from one of her bags and placed them on the bed. "They match the sheets." She grinned impishly at me as she saw me looking at the pillows.

"Uh huh," I said and then teased her. "No teddy bears as well?"

"Nah," she giggled. "Maybe I'll move them in next week, once I see how everything works out."

"Uh huh." I shook my head and laughed. "I'm hungry. Wanna grab a bite?"

"Yes." She nodded eagerly. "What're you making?"

"Oh." I paused. "I thought you would make something, now that you're here."

"What am I? A housewife?" She looked at me with wide eyes. "Here to cook your meals and service you?"

"I wouldn't say no." I winked at her and her jaw dropped. "But no, that's not why you're here." I shook my head. "And I was joking about the food. I actually have stuff."

"Oh?"

"I bought some tomato soup at the deli last night and I have stuff for grilled cheese sandwiches. I remember you always loved soup and grilled cheese."

"Good memory." She smiled happily. "Sounds yummy. Let's go make 'em. I can help."

"Oh?"

"I'll heat the soup up." She laughed as we walked to the kitchen. "You can impress me with your grilled-cheese-making skills."

"Well, you know I have so many skills. I don't want to be showing off all of them."

"I think it's okay." She patted me on the arm. "I think you won't get a big head."

"I'm not going to say what I was going to say because you're a lady." I winked at her and she punched me in the arm.

"You're a pervert."

"And you love that about me."

"Maybe, maybe not," she said, her eyes softening as she looked at me. I laughed, my eyes taking in every detail of her face. The curve of her lips, so luscious and pink, the twinkle in her eye as she gazed at me in something akin to delight. Her skin was glowing and I could see just how happy she was. In fact, my whole body could feel it, because I felt the same way. We were just so at ease. Our spirits flowed together. It felt natural being with Mila. She was the only person I ever truly felt comfortable with. She made me feel like I could just be me. All of me, in every way. There was no facade. There was no trying. I could tell my goofy jokes. I could be rude, fun, silly, sad, quiet, whatever and she always got me. I'd never really thought about that before. I'd never really thought about just how easy it was with her.

"What do you want to do later?"

"I don't know." She shrugged. "Maybe talk about the business stuff?" She made a face. "Exactly what I'm doing as your four-week fiancée?" she asked me and looked into my eyes so earnestly that I felt my heart stop for a few seconds. It always came back to this. While sometimes I could forget exactly what we were doing, I knew I could never really forget. Not when the truth of the matter was so very dark and deep. My heart sank and I could feel my energy sapping as I realized that this comfortable feeling with Mila might soon be something of the past.

"Eh, do we want to talk about business?" I asked her lightly, my heart sinking.

"I guess not." She shrugged. "What about Cody and Barbie? Do you know what's going on with them?"

"What do you mean what's going on?" I opened the fridge door to take out the bread, butter and assortment of cheeses.

"Are they still seeing each other?" she asked curiously.

"I didn't know they were seeing each other," I said carefully, studying the cheese packets closely.

"Well, they had sex." Mila sounded disgusted. "So I'm curious if that's still going on? I wanted to have Cody and Sally over for dinner, but not if he's going to bring that ho."

"Are you trying to match-make them?" I looked at Mila then. "Are you sure that's a good idea? I mean, Cody seems to be all over the place right now."

"Sally is too good for Cody." Mila made a face. "He's my brother and I love him, but when he had sex with Barbie, I could have killed him. She's such a skanky bitch."

"Mila." I shook my head at her.

"What?" She glared at me. "It's true. And I blame you for bring-ing her that weekend."

"It's not my fault that Cody slept with her." I really didn't want to talk about this. The more we talked about Barbie, the worse I felt. Mila didn't know how I really knew Barbie and, at this point, even if

I wanted to tell her I couldn't. There had been too many lies. Too much deceit. I knew that Mila wouldn't understand, especially seeing as I couldn't tell her everything that was going on. But I also knew that she would find out eventually. Eventually the truth would come out and everything around me would come crashing down.

My stomach churned as I thought about how Mila would react when she learned the truth. I could already see the pain and hurt in her eyes, maybe even anger and hatred. She'd never forgive me. That I knew for sure. And I didn't know if I'd ever forgive myself either. But I'd come so far. Too far. I was in it now. I was a man of my word. I had to follow through.

I wondered then, if I could go back in time, if I would still have agreed to the plan. At the time, it had seemed quite harmless. I hadn't thought that it was anything more than a business transaction, but then I hadn't been thinking with anything other than my head. Things had changed now. There was a part of me that couldn't stop thinking about how much I was hurting Mila and she didn't even know. I was ashamed of myself. I was a predator, taking what I wanted without any regard to my prey. I was the top of the food chain. I was king. And I didn't like who I was with all that power. I was a despot. A despicable person.

Yet, I was still able to forget. I was still able to be with Mila and pretend. Because when I was with Mila, I did forget. All I thought about was how easy and good it felt to be with her. She was so genuine, so sweet, so loving. I froze as I thought about that. She was loving. Too loving. I knew she was falling deeper and deeper for me. She possibly still had a crush on me. Still felt she was in love with me. I liked that, but I didn't. I didn't want her to fall in love with me. I didn't want her to think that I was something that I wasn't. Falling in love with me would only break her heart a second time. I couldn't do that to her. I wanted to be selfish. I wanted to feel her love. Oh, how her love filled me up. When I was lying in bed late at night, sometimes I would just picture her smile and the look in her eyes as she leaned over to hug me and kiss me and it would make me warm. It would make me feel things that I'd never imagined feeling before. Sometimes those feelings made me feel uncomfortable. If they happened in the day, I banished them. But late at night, when the lights were out and it was quiet, I could pretend it was all a dream world. A dream-world fantasy and I'd let myself enjoy it. I'd let myself just soak it all in. And in those moments, I felt alive, truly alive. It was only in the morning that I'd be angry at myself.

"TJ, are you paying attention to me?" Mila poked me in the arm.

"Sorry, what?" I gave her an awkward look, not having heard a word she'd said. "I was thinking about something."

"Not about Barbie, I hope," she said jealously and I tried not to grin.

"Maybe I'll think about Barbie while you think of your ex-boyfriends."

"You're an asshole." She glared at me.

"Am I?" I asked her and leaned over and kissed her on the lips. "Let's not talk about Barbie anymore. She's tiresome."

"So does that mean she's banished from our lives forever?" Mila asked eagerly, her eyes wide and a huge smile on her face.

"Yeah," I said softly, not wanting to lie, but not knowing what to say.

"So Cody is no longer seeing her?"

"Cody is no longer seeing her." I nodded. That was true. Cody had no interest in her other than from that night. Though we hadn't really spoken about it. We hadn't spoken about much since my fake engagement to Mila. Not that he knew it was fake. He was pissed at me for having kept our "relationship" a secret for so long. I didn't know what to tell him. I couldn't tell him the truth either. And that added to my hurt. We'd been best friends for so long and I felt that I was ruining everything with my actions.

"At least Cody grew some brains. It's a pity it happened before he became a douchebag."

"I think he did Sally a favor," I said, sticking up for him. "At least she knows now that he likes to get around."

"I don't think that makes her feel better." Mila rolled her eyes. "Men change when they're in love."

"So you think Cody would have stopped sleeping around if he was in love with Sally?"

"Yes." She nodded. "That's what love is all about."

"Okay." I tried to hide a grin.

"What? It's true. When people are in true love, they don't mess around."

"Uhm, okay. True love, huh?" I nodded.

"Whatever." She looked pissed. "I mean, it's not like you're going to mess around on me, right?" Her eyes searched mine.

"Well, we're not in true love, so technically I can, right?" I responded without thinking and I saw her face drop. I immediately regretted my choice of words, but then realized that perhaps they were the best words I could have uttered. I mean, I had to disabuse Mila of the idea that this was ever going to be some picture-perfect love story. That wasn't how our story was going to go down.

"Yeah, we're not in love." Mila shrugged, her voice void of emotion as she looked back up at me with a disinterested expression. "We can do whatever we want."

"Well, no, we can't." I frowned. "As per the contract, we both will remain faithful for the duration of the engagement." I pursed my lips. "We don't want anyone on the board to have any inkling that this isn't a love match, and if you're flirting around with a bunch of other men, it's going to be hard to convince them of that fact."

"Yeah, 'cause I'm the person that's going to be flirting around." She stepped back. "Excuse me, I need to go to the restroom."

"Okay." I nodded. "Do you need anything?"

"Nope," she said as she walked away and I'm pretty sure I heard her mumbling under her breath something like, "I need you to not be an insensitive asshole." I didn't ask her to speak up, though. She was entitled to her thoughts and feelings. In fact, this is what I wanted. I wanted her to enjoy having fun with me, but I didn't want her to fall in love with me. We both needed to remember what this was about. This was for fun and excitement. This was for me to fulfill my obligation and duties for the promise I'd made. I sighed as I realized that I'd made a deal with the devil and I wondered if I was going to burn in hell for the rest of my life. As I stood there, feeling uneasy, I knew that that would be a light punishment for the game I was playing. A very light punishment indeed.

Chapter Five

TJ

Two Years Ago

"I WANT A RELATIONSHIP." HEIDI'S whine was irritating my ears and I tried not to frown at her. "I want to be your girlfriend."

"I told you I'm not looking for a girlfriend," I said matter-of-factly and checked my watch to make sure that I hadn't missed the beginning of the game.

"TJ Walker, did you just check your watch?" Heidi pouted. "Do you have somewhere to be that's more important than this conversation?"

"Honestly?" I asked her, wondering if she realized just how honest I was.

"Yes," she said, her eyes looking into mine in a surprised expression.

"Okay, well, I told Cody I'd watch the game with him tonight and kickoff is in twenty minutes, so I kinda have to leave soon."

"But you just got here an hour ago." She looked incredulous. "What was this? A booty call?"

"I'd have to be getting some booty for that." I winked at her, but she didn't laugh.

"All you want me for is sex," she said slowly as if that was just dawning on her. I wasn't sure why she was so surprised. I wasn't sure why any girl was surprised when they realized I didn't want a relationship. I never told them anything different.

"I like you, Heidi," I said, giving her a weak smile. "I'm just not in a position to be in a relationship right now."

"What position is that, TJ?" She growled, starting to sound angry. "The position of being an adult? The last time I checked, you were one."

"I don't want a relationship," I said honestly. "And if I did, it wouldn't be with you." I shook my head to myself as the words came out. They were true, but I knew they were hurtful.

"You're a dirty rotten bastard." She glared at me and her eyes looked glossy. That was the first time a woman had called me that and to be quite honest, I agreed with her. I stared back at her and wondered if I could make it out of her apartment before she started crying. I really didn't want to have to waste time comforting her.

"I really liked you, TJ," she said plaintively, reaching forward and grabbing my hands. "I can help you. You can tell me anything, TJ. I can help you get through your issues."

"I don't have any issues." I sighed and pulled my hands back. I was starting to feel irritated. Heidi really didn't get it. If she wanted me to stay, there was basically only one thing she could do right now and that was to pull my zipper down and take me into her mouth, and even then I'd be resistant to staying, now that I knew she wanted a relationship and was in the "pleading for it" stage. There was nothing worse than a normally confident and attractive woman begging me for a relationship, when she knew I didn't want that. I wasn't sure what it was about women that made them think that they could sleep with a man enough times to make them commit. Didn't they realize that a man wanted more than some ass to commit to someone? So many times, I wanted to tell these women that just because they let me fuck them up the ass or in some back alleyway, that wasn't making me respect them. And the attempts to pull out my cock and suck me under the table at restaurants were too numerous to count. I wasn't sure what manual women read that made them believe that sex was a way to a man's heart. But it needed to be updated.

"So you're just going to leave?" She pouted at me. "That's it?" Tears started to roll down her cheeks and I sighed. I really didn't have time for this. "You're just going to leave me like this?" She pursed her lips and I felt her hands reach down to my zipper. "I want you to stay, TJ." She slipped her fingers inside my boxers and I felt her slightly cold and trembling fingers on my shaft.

"I see," I said, and I contemplated staying for another hour, when I heard my phone beeping. I grabbed it from my pocket and read the text message from Cody: *Dude, just a heads up, Mila and Sally are coming over as well, so don't plan on bringing any weed over.* I stared at the text, pulled Heidi's hand out of my pants and took a step back.

"Sorry, Heidi, it's just not going to work out," I said, giving her a quick nod and walked over to her front door. "Bye," I said as I opened the front door and hurried out of her apartment. My mind was off of Heidi as soon as I opened my car door. There was only one woman who had any part of my mind. And that was the one woman I would never let myself have.

Present Day

THE SMELL OF HONEYSUCKLE HIT me as soon as I opened my front door. It wafted through the air and surprised me as I made my way into the hallway. The smell was unfamiliar, but sweet and homey. My apartment was slowly becoming a real home and it was a weird feeling to suddenly realize that.

"Honey, I'm home," I called out, feeling my mood lifting as I looked around the living room. Mila had added a few homey touches to my place since she'd moved in a week ago and I was pleasantly surprised at how cozy my place seemed. Everything had been going smoothly and I was enjoying coming home to her. It almost seemed like I was in some sort of movie, with the happy wife and the perfect life. All we were missing were the kids and a Golden Retriever. Oh and living in true happiness and bliss, of course. Our happiness was predicated on a lie, but I was trying to forget that fact.

"Hey." Mila's voice sounded happy as she came running out of the kitchen towards me. "You're home." She ran up to me and gave me a big hug and a kiss on the lips, her cheeks a rosy pink, and her eyes sparkling in happiness.

"I am," I said and kissed her back, my heart feeling odd as I gazed at her. "I see you did some shopping."

"Just some small stuff." She laughed as she gazed around the apartment and realized just how much she'd transformed my place. There were flowers everywhere and lots of new knick-knacks, like vases and little pots and containers with candles and candy. She'd also added some new art to my walls, bright colorful Picasso prints that popped out and made the room seem grander. There was a new throw blanket on the couch that she'd gotten; it was made of alpaca wool and it was gray and soft and even though I didn't know what an alpaca was, I enjoyed the feeling of it covering us when we lay on the couch together. I was a man and would never admit to it, but I liked the small luxuries that she'd brought to my life.

"I have a new couch coming as well." She bit down on her lower lip and looked up at me with wide eyes.

"You have a new couch coming?" I asked her with a grin, laughing at her joke.

"I'm not joking, TJ." She giggled. "Don't be mad."

"You seriously have a new couch coming?" I asked her, my eyes searching hers and I could tell from her expression that she was dead serious. "What's wrong with my couch?"

"Leather? Dark, sticky leather?" She made a face. "So unattractive."

"It's comfortable." I shrugged, still not quite believing that she'd actually purchased a new couch. That was a huge purchase and I really felt taken aback. I'd never expected Mila to get that comfortable in my place. I liked it and hated it both at the same time.

"It's not cute, though." She wrinkled her nose as she looked over at my most prized piece of furniture. "And there are no throw pillows."

"It's soft enough to not need throw pillows," I said and looked at my couch longingly. "Plus, we have an alpaca throw blanket now. Isn't that enough?"

"No, TJ." She giggled and shook her head.

"When will it be leaving my abode?" I asked mournfully, wondering if I could hold some sort of funeral for the couch before it left. And the funeral would consist of us having sex on the couch in multiple positions. That would partially make up for her replacing it.

"Hopefully this weekend." She looked at me nervously. "I told the store we'd pay extra for a fast delivery of the new sectional."

"You did, did you?" I raised an eyebrow at her. What had happened to the girl who was too timid to use my credit card? She'd obviously disappeared. I was going to make a comment, but I stopped myself. I had a feeling if I made a joke, she'd take it self-consciously and then maybe she really would stop using the card. Which I didn't want. I liked that she felt comfortable enough with me now to not call me every time she wanted to charge twenty dollars for some silly purchase. I had plenty of money and I was happy for her to use it.

"Yeah, I wanted it to arrive in time for the dinner party. Make our home look more cozy to everyone." She gave me a winning smile.

"Are you saying our home isn't cozy?" I asked her and she smirked at me. I saw her smiling and realized that I'd said "our home," as opposed to "my home." It was weird that I was starting to think of this as our home now. I wasn't sure how it was going to feel when she moved out. How cozy and homey all her little knick-knacks would feel once she was gone. I'd most probably pack them up into a box and take them to Goodwill. I wouldn't want to be reminded of her time here. Not once everything came out. It would remind me too much of all I'd lost.

"What do you think, TJ?" she said and then shrieked and ran back to the kitchen.

"What's going on?" I followed behind her and watched as she hurriedly opened the oven door.

"I'm roasting some potatoes and I didn't want them to burn." She pulled out a tray from the oven and placed them on top of the stove. "You like herb-roasted potatoes, right?" She turned to me with a sweet smile. "I remember you used to scarf them down when you'd come over. My mom used to call you the potato monster."

"She did, didn't she?" I laughed as I remembered all of the meals that I'd eaten with her family. I'd never thought that one day, we'd be here and she'd be cooking for me. "Her potatoes were the bomb."

"Yeah, so are mine, though." Mila laughed.

"As long as you don't burn them." I winked at her. "Your mom would never burn them."

"Shh, you." She grabbed a towel and swatted me with it as she laughed. "If you keep insulting me, you won't get any dinner."

"Hmm, let me hear what's for dinner, first." I raised an eyebrow at her. "Then I'll decide if I want to keep insulting you."

"You're incorrigible." She giggled. "I'm making a roast chicken, with roast potatoes, gravy, Brussels sprouts and carrots."

"Sounds delicious." I licked my lips.

"And an apple pie with ice cream for dessert."

"Okay, I'm sold. No more insults." I paused. "For the day."

"TJ Walker." She laughed. "Come on now."

"Come on now, what?" I grinned. "What are you going to make for the dinner party?"

"I'm not sure yet, but I was thinking of grilling some steaks."

"Steaks are always good." I nodded. "Who's coming, again?"

"Sally and Cody," she said as she closed the oven door and went to the fridge.

"What about your parents?" I asked. "And Nonno."

"Nah, didn't invite them," she said with a shake of her head. "We can have them over soon."

"Have you spoken to Nonno recently?" I asked hesitantly.

"Not really." She shook her head again. "I've been busy."

"So you've not seen him, either?" I frowned, my heart feeling heavy. I was the one who was keeping her from him.

"No, I'll see him soon." She smiled at me. "I've been busy trying to turn this place into a real home. Maybe we'll have my folks over and your dad."

"Yeah." Over my dead body.

"And is your dad seeing anyone? We can invite his latest paramour as well." She giggled. "I swear that man goes through women like some women go through underwear."

"I'm not sure what he's doing right now or if he's still dating the same lady, or one or more ladies." My mind immediately flew to Barbie and I could feel myself growing uncomfortable. What would Mila say if I told her that Barbie was sleeping with my dad? If I just dropped it casually into the conversation like it was no big thing, would she react as if it were no big thing? Would she smile and say, "Oh really? That's funny. Wow, Barbie really gets around." I half-smiled as that thought crossed my mind. Yeah, right. There was no way that my Mila would ever act that calmly. She'd go quiet first, thinking about what I'd said and then when she processed everything and realized she'd heard correctly, she would lose it. Maybe she'd start shouting. Maybe she'd cry. But I knew that she'd be anything but calm and accepting. That was not a small lie that I could just sweep under the rug.

"Aw, yeah, who can keep up with him," she said as she took out a bag of Brussels sprouts from the fridge. "Do you have any kosher salt?" she asked me as she started rinsing the sprouts in the sink and scrubbing them.

"I have salt." I shrugged. "I have no idea what kosher salt is. I'm not Jewish."

"Oh, TJ." She rolled her eyes at me. "Pass me the olive oil and black pepper and all the different salts that you have. I'll check."

"All what different salts?" I laughed. "I have one regular salt and that's it."

"Fine." She sighed. "Just pass me that as well, then."

"Yes, boss." I saluted her and she laughed. "What's all this for?"

"The Brussels sprouts," she said and held up the bowl she was holding. "I'm going to roast them with the seasonings. It will be delicious. Trust me."

"I'm sure everything you make is delicious," I said. "Just like you."

"Flattery will get you everywhere." She winked at me. "Joke, it will get you nowhere."

"Damn it." I grabbed her around the waist and pulled her towards me. "I want it to get me any and everywhere."

"Sorry about your luck." She giggled as she wriggled away from me.

"Oh yeah?" I leaned down and nibbled on the top of her ear as I brought her ass back up against me so she could feel my hardness.

"TJ, I'm cooking."

"So?" I laughed and kept my arms around her, moving them up to her breasts and gently squeezed them. "Didn't you know that kitchen sex was good for you?"

"Oh?" She giggled again and she moaned as I squeezed her nipples.

"Yeah, it's like a workout before pigging out. Burn those calories early."

"Hmm, are you calling me fat?" she said and then laughed as I froze. "Got ya."

"Mila," I murmured, laughing with her as I turned her around to face me. "I don't care how fat you are."

"That's not a good response." She made a face at me and I leaned down to kiss her long and hard, sliding my tongue into her mouth. She tasted sweet and she melted into me, kissing me back eagerly. Her hands flew to my hair and I held her face, caressing her cheeks as we kissed. I felt happy, calm, and like this was how it should be. The moment was everything that I'd never thought I could ever have. It was the stuff of fairy tales and, while I knew fairy tales were fiction, I wasn't going to ruin the moment. I was just going to live in it. The nightmare would be here soon enough.

Right then my phone beeped and I grabbed it from my pocket to see who was texting me. The text was from my dad and it made my heart freeze.

"I need an update. Chinese want the deal to go through ASAP. Do you have the power of attorney papers?"

I deleted the text quickly, put the phone back into my pocket and held Mila close to me again. Hell on Earth was going to be here sooner than I'd hoped.

Chapter Six

Mila

I WALKED DOWN THE STREET with a wide smile on my face. I wasn't sure why I was so happy. Maybe it was something about the day. The sky was a deep azure blue, with nary a cloud to be seen, the sun was out and shining warmly, the trees were tall and proud and the fall colors of the leaves were beautiful: warm reds, deep browns, dancing yellows and secretive greens beckoned to me. I smiled again as I saw two birds flying from one tree to another, seeming to take the same path down the street as I was. My heart felt full and I was happy.

I knew that most of my happiness stemmed from the fact that I was on the way to meet TJ for dinner. It was scary how excited and happy he made me. And I didn't even have to be with him. Just the knowledge that I'd see him soon was enough for me. I just liked being around him. That was all I needed to feel warm and content. I didn't even have to talk to him or touch him. Just knowing that he was there was enough for me. He filled my heart and spirit in a way that I didn't understand.

It scared me, in a way, knowing how much power he had over me. I didn't want to think about what would happen when I no longer got to spend so much time with him. I didn't want to think about not being with him.

Even though our relationship—well, engagement—was fake, it didn't matter to me. It didn't matter because I was still getting to know him better. I was still getting to see parts of him I'd never seen before. His vulnerabilities, the things that made him hurt, pause, think. There was a side to TJ that I'd never known existed. I'd always thought he was this tough, handsome guy. Full of life and vitality. A guy who took everything in stride. Nothing ever got him down. That's what I used to think. I mean, I knew that his dad wasn't the most paternalistic figure in his life. I knew that had to have affected him in some way. And the fact that his mother had died when he was so young. I'd thought about it, but had never really placed any real emotion or depth into those thoughts. Now, I wondered just how much his childhood had affected him. Who was TJ Walker behind the façade? I was still trying to figure that out.

He was darker inside than I'd thought. There was a barrier there, some layer of hurt, some deep emotion hidden inside of him. And it fascinated me. I wanted to know his full story. And I wanted to fix him. I wanted my love to fix him.

I shook my head at myself as I continued walking, nearing the restaurant. I knew I was living in the clouds. Life wasn't like the movies. I wasn't going to be able to fix him and make him fall in love with me. Stuff like that just didn't happen. Least of all to people like me. But that didn't stop me from hoping. That didn't stop me from wishing that I could somehow figure out what made him tick and in doing so make him fall head over heels in love with me. That would be amazing. Not realistic, but definitely amazing.

I giggled as I walked into the restaurant, feeling light-hearted and giddy as I felt my heart racing. I was about to see TJ and that always made me feel awesome. I used to live for seeing him every few months; now I got to see him every day.

The host greeted me with a big smile. "Good evening, ma'am. Do you have a reservation?"

"Yes—well, not me." I laughed. "I'm meeting someone here. I think he has the reservation."

"What's his name?" He smiled at me warmly. "Let's see if he's here yet."

"TJ Walker," I said, grinning.

"I see his reservation, but he hasn't checked in as yet. We can definitely seat you while you wait, though. Would you like that, madam?"

"Mila." I smiled at him sweetly. "And yes, please, that would be amazing. Thank you."

"Oh, you're very welcome." He nodded and looked back down at his podium. "One moment, please."

"Oh, of course." I smoothed my skirt down and pulled out my lipstick so that I could reapply it. I wasn't sure why I felt so nervous, but I wanted to look pretty for TJ. Like, really pretty. I wanted him to walk in and look at me and think to himself, *Wow, Mila is just gorgeous. How did I get so lucky to be having dinner with her?* I mean, it was a pipedream—he'd never really given me a look like that before—but that didn't stop me from hoping.

"This way, ma'am." He came towards me. "Just follow me."

"Sure." I smiled and followed behind him. We approached a table and as the maître d' was about to pull my chair out, a handsome man jumped up from the table next to mine and pulled it out for me.

"Good evening." He gave me a wide smile and a wink as he stood behind me.

"Evening." I smiled at him, feeling a bit shy as he pushed my chair in. "You didn't have to do that."

"I see a beautiful woman and I can't stop myself," he said. "I'm Will, by the way."

"Mila." I held my hand out to him.

"A beautiful name for a beautiful girl."

"Oh." I blushed, not knowing what to say.

"I'll just leave the wine menu with you," the maître d' said and beamed at us both as he backed away.

"Dining alone?" Will asked me hopefully, his eyes a piercing navy blue in his handsome face.

I shook my head. "No, I'm waiting on someone."

"Would you like company while you wait?" he asked, showing his perfect white teeth. His dark gold hair was cut perfectly and shone on top of his head as he waited for my answer. I blushed again, still not knowing what to say. I was taken aback that this gorgeous man was asking to sit with me and was flirting with me.

"Oh, you don't have to do that." I shook my head again and stared at his perfect navy, pinstriped suit. I was still in internal shock that he was talking to me. I wasn't used to men just coming up to me; especially not distinguished, handsome men like him.

"It would be my pleasure." He took a seat next to me. "I'm dining alone, so I'd be happy to keep you company until your girlfriend gets here."

"Oh, it's a male friend." I blushed, wondering why I hadn't said fiancé. Maybe because it felt like too much of a lie.

"I guess that was pretty obvious that I was fishing, huh?" He laughed.

"Fishing?" I asked dumbly, not sure what he was saying.

"For information. You know, to see if you're single." He leaned forward and adjusted his tie. "Though that would've been too much to ask. Have a beautiful single woman just fall into my lap."

"Oh, ha ha." I laughed uncomfortably. I'd never had a guy come on to me so strongly before.

"So, not single?" he asked more directly, his eyes light as he chuckled.

"Um, yes, no—kinda." I laughed at the confusion on his face. "It's kinda complicated."

"I can work with complicated." He winked and then leaned back. "And in case you were wondering, I'm single." He grinned. "Would you like a glass of wine?"

"Oh. I shouldn't." I shook my head, feeling slightly dazed and confused, and a little proud of myself. I had to be looking pretty good if this handsome man was spending so much time flirting with me and offering to buy me a glass of wine.

"Don't you drink?" he asked curiously.

"Oh, I do, but like I said, I'm waiting on someone."

"He's not a very good someone, though, is he?" Will looked at me and frowned. "He's got you sitting here waiting on him."

"I'm sure he just got caught up at work," I said with a small smile. "He's a busy guy."

"I'm a very busy guy, but look where I am right now," he said seriously, and I started to feel my heart sinking a little. What was he trying to say? That TJ didn't respect me or my time? He was only five minutes late. But then as I thought about it, I wondered if he was late when he went on real dates. I bet he was early for women he wanted to go out with. Women he really liked. I was just his fake fiancée, the girl he was fucking. He didn't really care about me. I wondered how he treated the women he really cared for. I could feel my stomach churning as my thoughts immediately turned negative.

"Hey, you okay, Mila?" Will leaned forward. "I didn't mean to hit a nerve."

"Sorry, what?" I asked him, blinking, trying to get rid of the heavy feeling that had hit me.

"Maybe work was just really busy," he said. "I mean, if he has you waiting around a lot, maybe he doesn't care as much as you hope. A woman like you deserves a man that's going to put her above everything else."

"Thank you," I said with a small smile, looking at my watch and realizing that TJ was actually fifteen minutes late instead of five minutes late.

"I know you don't know me," Will said, and I watched as he pulled his wallet out of his pocket. "But if it doesn't work out with this guy, or you want to talk to me or let me take you out for a drink, give me a call at this number." He pulled a card out and handed it to me. "I'd love to take you for a drink. Show you how a gentleman treats his lady. I, for one, wouldn't have you waiting."

"Oh, wow, thanks." I held his card in my hand and looked down at it awkwardly. How did one respond to that? And where was TJ?

"Mila." TJ's voice was loud behind me and it made me jump.

"TJ?" I said, looking at him with narrowed eyes and a red face, like I'd been caught red-handed with my hand in the cookie jar.

"What's going on?" He frowned and looked at the card in my hand and then at Will.

"I was just keeping Mila company." Will stood up, nodded at TJ and then looked back down at me. "It was a pleasure making your acquaintance tonight, Mila. Please call me if I can ever take you out for a drink."

"Thank you," I squeaked out and I could feel TJ's eyes on me. I looked up at him and gave him a quick smile, but he just frowned at me, his eyes narrowed as he watched Will going back to his seat.

"Making new friends already?" he said as he sat down. "Looking for someone new?"

"TJ, we were just talking." I rolled my eyes at him. "Don't being stupid."

"I'm not being stupid." He pursed his lips. "Do you know what you want to order or did you even bother to look at the menu."

"I think I'm going to get a steak. And lobster. And oysters. And caviar. And lots of champagne," I said sweetly and then smiled. "You can afford it."

"Funny," he said as he looked at me, but I saw that he wasn't able to keep a smile off of his face.

"That's me, one funny girl." I grinned at him, determined to not let him ruin my good mood. I stared at his handsome face, so serious as he sat there in his smart business suit. His eyes looked at me searchingly, with a glint of judgment as if he were telling me off for talking with Will. A part of me was delighted that he appeared to be jealous. Another part of me was annoyed that he was going to be acting like a bit of an ass, just because I was being friendly to another guy. It wasn't like I wanted the other guy. All I could think about was TJ.

"Yes, one funny, sexy girl," he said and I felt his hand reach down and grab my knee under the table and his fingers started running up and down my calf.

"What're you doing, TJ?" My eyes widened as I gazed at him.

"Nothing." He grinned as his fingers moved up my legs again and he pushed against my inner thigh to gain access. I squeezed my legs together closer in response.

"TJ." I pursed my lips at him. "Stop it."

"Stop what?" he asked, a wry smile on his face as he pushed harder between my legs and they fell apart slightly. His fingers took immediate advantage of the movement and they ran up and down my inner thigh under my skirt. I held my breath as they drew dangerously high.

"You know what?" I frowned at him. "You just got here. Stop it."

"Stop what?" He laughed and then looked away from me as a waitress approached the table.

"Hi, I'm Madeline. I'll be taking care of you today."

"Why, thank you," TJ said as he grinned at her. "I do enjoy being taken care of."

"Then I'm glad I'm here." Madeline flirted back with him and I watched as she tossed her long raven hair back and pushed her ample bust forward. I glanced up at her face with a slight glare and felt my resolve failing as I looked at her face properly. She was gorgeous, her skin was smooth and her eyes were a sparkling, vibrant blue. She had fine features and perfect lips. And she was petite. She looked like the perfect woman. I felt jealousy searing through me as I gazed at her staring at TJ and TJ staring back into her eyes with a wide, genuine smile. His fingers were still on my legs, but were moving in a haphazard fashion as he glanced at her. I could feel my stomach churning and I felt my good mood vanishing.

"Would you like a drink, sir?" she asked, her voice melodic.

"What would you recommend?" He leaned back and moved his hand away from my leg.

"What is sir into?" She leaned closer to him, leaning down and opening the menu in front of him. Her hair hung down, surrounding her face, and she looked into his eyes with a sweet, eager smile.

"Whatever you think I'd like." His eyes teased her and I watched as he licked his lips slowly. I froze at the obvious flirtation between them. My breath was coming fast and my stomach was in knots as I just sat there being ignored.

"I think I'll have a glass of water," I said, finally speaking up, and the girl straightened and looked at me with a sweet and pitying look.

"Sure." She nodded. "Still or sparkling?"

"Still, thanks." I bit down on my lower lip, feeling like I wanted to cry.

"Okay." She nodded and then looked back over at TJ. "And have you decided?"

"I'll have a whiskey, neat."

"Brand?" She grinned at him.

"Surprise me," he said and she just giggled like a little schoolgirl. I could feel my face flaming. I was embarrassed, upset, jealous, annoyed, and pissed off. How could TJ flirt with this girl in front of me, like that? I guess it was the reality check I needed. He just wasn't interested in me, at all.

"Okay, I'll do that," she said, tossing her hair back again and lightly touching him on the shoulder. I looked away and tried to ignore the feelings telling me to slap her. She was the sort of girl I knew was used to getting what she wanted based on her looks, and I was pretty sure that she wanted TJ and that she didn't care that I was sitting here with him. She probably thought I was his secretary and not his girlfriend. Though, technically, I wasn't his girlfriend. I was just the girl he was fucking and pretending to be his fake fiancée.

I watched as she walked away and then looked over at TJ, who was looking at his watch. He then looked up at me with a slightly cold expression. "So, think of any exes today, or were you just hoping to meet a new guy to try in bed?"

"What?" I snapped at him, annoyed. How was he going to turn this on me?

"You seem to work pretty fast." He shrugged and I felt his hand on my leg again, even more aggressive than before. "I'm just wondering if you're looking to compare fuck buddies or something."

"What's that supposed to mean?" I said, my voice growing louder. Where was this coming from?

"Just that you always seem to be thinking of another guy or chatting one up," he snapped.

"What guys have I ever been chatting up?" I snapped back at him.

"Aside from that twat that was at the table with you?"

"We were talking."

"Is that all you wanted?" he asked, his fingers pushing their way up to my panties. I felt his finger rubbing against me roughly and I gasped as my legs unconsciously spread to give him better access.

"Stop," I said, my eyes watering as I felt his fingers starting to move into my panties.

"Is this what you want?" he said as his finger rubbed my clit under the table. "It feels like it," he said as he continued to rub me. I knew I was wet down there and I hated myself for it. How could this be turning me on?

"No," I said and snapped my legs shut.

"Okay," he said and withdrew his finger from my panties and then moved his hand back down my leg slowly. I watched as his hand made its way back to the table and then he placed a finger into his mouth and sucked on it slowly. "Sure seems like you wanted it." He looked at me; his eyes hollow as I watched him. My face was hot with shame and I looked away from him. Why was he being like this to me?

Madeline made her way back to the table. "Here's your water," she said, placing the glass in front of me. "And your whiskey, sir." She placed it in front of him and stood back to watch him. "I can't wait to see if you enjoy it."

I wanted to shout at her to "just move it, bitch," but I didn't. I just sat there, feeling even more inferior and cheap.

"Let's see." TJ sat back, a wide smile on his face for the waitress, his eyes looking at her admiringly. Gone was the cold, calculating look. And in its place, instead, was an interested, happy face. My heart dropped as I watched him pick up the glass and take a sip. He swallowed slowly and then he looked at Madeline in approval. "Very, very nice. You have good taste."

"Thank you." She blushed and ran her hand through her hair. "I'll be back to take your food order in a few minutes."

"Sounds great," TJ said. "Though maybe I'll let you pick for me."

"You'd trust me for that?" she asked with a huge smile.

"I'd trust you with a lot more than that." He winked at her and then I saw him give me a quick look, as if to see if I was paying attention. His eyes met mine, and he looked at me and studied my face for a second before I turned my face away from him.

"Okay, I'll be back," Madeline said and I watched as she and TJ exchanged one last smile. The look on TJ's face was one of teasing happiness and it made my heart fall heavily. The happiness and excitement that I'd been feeling earlier in the day was completely gone. I'd been fooling myself, telling myself that TJ wanted me and was falling for me as well. This was nothing to him. I was nothing to him and I never would be.

TJ DROPPED ME OFF AFTER a very quiet dinner and said he had to go back to the office to do some work. I just nodded and got out of the car without even looking at him. I felt completely broken and dejected. My spirits were low and all I wanted to do was call Sally. I couldn't deal with this. I couldn't deal with TJ treating me like this. I couldn't deal with being around him and not really having him.

It had never really hit me until that moment that there was never going to be a happily-ever-after with TJ. He just wasn't into me in that way. All he wanted was sex and to have a good time. I couldn't even be mad. He'd never given me any reason to think any other way.

My body flashed hot and cold as I walked into his apartment and I immediately walked to his bathroom and started running a bath. All I wanted to do was soak and cry and get it out. Then I'd call Sally. Right now, I needed hot water over me.

I took off my shoes and started to take off my skirt and under-wear. Tears started streaming down my face as I got undressed. I grabbed my phone and clicked on my music icon so I could listen to some James Bay while I had my bath. I loved his music, it was emotional, and while I knew I should listen to something hard and more rock-like to get over my depressed state, I couldn't bring myself to do it.

I stepped into the bath and squealed as the hot water burned me, but I didn't jump out. I deserved the pain for being such a dumbass. I slowly started to sit down as the water continued to sting me. And then the song, "If You Ever Want to Be in Love" started playing through my phone. The tears came even faster as I finally submerged myself in the water and sat down; the tears were both for my heartache and the scalding the water was giving me.

I leaned back and closed my eyes as I let the water crash over me. The tears streamed down my face and all I could picture was TJ's face as he'd smiled at the waitress—how happy and light-hearted he'd been as he'd innocently flirted with her. I'd seen the look he'd given her. It was fun, flirty, carefree and she'd responded in the same way. I couldn't ever remember him ever giving me that look. When I was younger he'd looked at me as his best friend's younger sister who was dorky, and he'd teased me relentlessly. Sometimes he'd looked at me with more emotion, when he'd listened to me talk about exams or heartaches or other silly things that had bothered me. He'd given me hugs, been caring, but he'd never given me a look of instant attraction, of love, of real interest.

And now, now that we were older and doing things I'd only hoped we'd be doing, some of his looks had changed. I'd seen lust in his eyes. I'd seen bare-naked want, but I'd not seen that innocent attraction, the admiration, the stirrings of a beginning love. I'd only fooled myself into thinking that we could have something real. He'd told me over and over again that this was a contract. He'd told me over and over he didn't do love. He'd reminded me that he wasn't the man for me. I wasn't sure why I hadn't listened to him.

Actually, that was a lie. I knew why I hadn't listened to him. Because my heart was holding on to a string attached to the moon and the stars. My heart was hoping that God would answer my prayers and that TJ would fall head over heels in love with me. I thought that God loved me. I thought he answered prayers. I'd been asking him for years to let TJ fall in love with me. I guess this was one prayer he wasn't interested in answering.

I reached over and grabbed my phone and called Sally. I needed to hear her voice. I needed her to tell me it was okay. I needed her to tell me that one day, I'd meet my Prince Charming. One day someone would love me as much as I loved them. Even if that someone wasn't TJ.

"Hello?" Sally answered the phone, her voice out of breath.

"Hey, you busy?" I hiccupped.

"Just got done jogging. What's going on?"

"Not much," I said, my voice barely able to work through the tears.

"Are you okay?" She sounded concerned. "What's going on, Mila?"

"I want to ask you a question," I said, my voice wobbly. "You need to answer me honestly, okay?"

"Okay," she said, her voice light. "What's the question?"

"Did you ever think I had a real chance at a real relationship with TJ?"

"What?" she said.

"You heard me. Did you ever really think TJ was interested in me?"

"You mean did I ever think he liked you before this?" she said, her words slow.

"Yeah, or did you ever think he would ever really want me? Like a man wants a woman he'll love for the rest of his life?"

"Why are you asking me this, Mila?" She sighed.

"Just answer me honestly. Answer me as a friend. Answer me as my best friend. And do me the honor of being straight. Not the best friend that wants to protect my feelings, but the best friend that wants to let her best friend know the truth."

"Mila." She sighed. "What is going on?"

"Answer me," I cried out. "Just answer the question." I sobbed for a few seconds. "Please."

"No," she said quietly, and her voice caught. "I'm sorry, Mila, but no, I never thought you and TJ would end up together, but that doesn't mean that . . ." Her voice trailed off as I screamed into the phone.

"Stop. Don't try and make me feel better. Just be honest with me. My heart is going to break either way. You trying to help my feelings isn't going to make me feel any better."

"You can do better than TJ, Mila," she said softly. "Where is this coming from?"

"I'll call you later," I said and hung up the phone quickly and then turned it off. All of a sudden, I felt tired, deathly tired. My body ached and I just wanted to lie down on the bed. I got up out of the bath and grabbed a towel. I dried myself for a few seconds and then waddled to the bedroom and walked over to the bed and collapsed onto it and started crying uncontrollably, TJ's handsome face filling my mind. I cried and cried until I started punching the pillow with my fists. I was so angry with myself. I felt so stupid. Like a fool and an idiot. How could I have put myself into this position? How could I have even thought for a minute that this was based on anything other than sex? TJ had never been interested in me. He'd never wooed me. He'd never come to me. Never asked me on a date. This was just a convenient hook-up for him. I wanted to scream at myself. Wanted to slap myself for thinking that he could ever love me.

What did I have to offer him? I wasn't beautiful. I didn't have a perfect body. I didn't look anything like the other girls he dated. I wasn't super smart. I wasn't sporty. I wasn't witty and intelligent. I didn't follow the news or international affairs. We had no real interests in common. I had nothing to offer him. He had the whole world to give a woman. I was nothing. Absolutely nothing.

My sobs were so loud that I didn't hear the front door opening. I didn't hear him walking towards the bedroom. I didn't hear him stop at the entrance to the bedroom door. I didn't hear him standing there, staring at me, crying my eyes out and punching the pillow like I was being killed or that someone in my life had died. I didn't hear anything. I just cried and cried because my heart was being pulled out of my body and I was slowly losing all will to ever feel good about myself or my life again. I felt like I was being broken in two. I felt like I was losing a part of myself in my despair. I'd never known what it was like to lose someone important before, but as I lay there crying, I

HELEN COOPER & J. S. COOPER

knew that I was losing a part of my heart. A part of my innocence was forever gone.

And then I heard him. And then I looked up, my heart pounding, my face red and splotchy. I froze as our eyes met and his face was a mask of worry and concern.

"Why are you crying, Mila?" TJ walked into the room, his face grim and twisted as he approached me, his eyes studying my face. "Who hurt you? What happened?"

"No one hurt me," I said as I looked away from him. How could I tell him that I was crying for myself because of him? Because he made me feel invisible? Because he'd never once looked at me in the way I'd seen him looking at the waitress in the restaurant? How could I tell him that I was crying because for once in my life I wanted to matter? I wanted to be the one someone wanted. I wanted to be the one admired. For all my laughter and plans, I was hurt inside. I was more than hurt. I was broken.

I'd tried to hide the fact that it hurt me that he didn't care for so many years. I'd lied to myself that I wasn't hurt and dejected. In my head and heart, I'd known that it would happen. I ignored the fact that he didn't pursue me. I made all these excuses to myself for the reasons why, when the real reason was in front of me. He just didn't care about me. Yeah, maybe he wanted to sleep with me, but I wasn't his *one*. I wasn't anything special. And knowing that, knowing that he'd never looked at me with that glint in his eyes that I'd seen when he'd looked at Madeline, killed me. It made me feel weak and empty and alone and there was nothing I could do to fix that feeling. There was nothing I could do to make him love me. There was nothing I could do to make him feel for me the way I felt for him.

I didn't understand why. I didn't understand how I could feel all these feelings, love him so much. I didn't understand why I would want him so much, when to him, I was nothing.

"Tell me why you're crying, Mila." He frowned as he sat next to me. "Who do I have to beat up?"

"No one. I'm fine." I gulped as he sat down on the bed and gingerly touched my shoulder.

"You're not fine." He lay down next to me and reached over to my face. "Tell me what's wrong, Mila. Please."

"Nothing is wrong." I kept my eyes down. How did you tell someone that their not loving you had broken you without seeming pathetic?

"Mila." His voice broke and I looked into his eyes. "What's going on?"

"Nothing, it doesn't matter." I tried to wipe my eyes. My whole being felt embarrassed and awkward.

"It matters to me," he said softly. "Please Mila, talk to me."

"You were mean to me tonight," I said softly, not knowing why I was letting the words out. "I was just waiting on you. And that guy approached me and you were mean."

"I didn't intend to be mean," he said stiffly.

"And then you were flirting with the waitress. I thought you were going to ask her out. It was so disrespectful." I looked down.

"I didn't realize I was flirting with her." He sighed. "Is that why you're crying?"

"I'm just emotional because I'm getting my period," I lied. I didn't want him to know I was devastated.

"I might have been flirting with the waitress because I wanted to make you jealous." He touched my cheek lightly and I looked over at him and he had a weird look on his face.

"Make me jealous?" I asked him, confused.

"I was looking forward to our dinner all day and then I walk in and see you flirting with some guy." He shrugged. "It made me upset."

"We weren't flirting."

"He wanted you."

"He was just being friendly."

"Guys are only friendly to women they want." He made a face. "He wanted you."

"I didn't want him."

"I acted irrationally, I'm sorry."

"It's okay." I took a huge breath and my heartbeat started to slow down as I calmed down a bit. So maybe he didn't think the waitress was his soul mate, after all. Though, I still thought it was pretty shitty that he'd been flirting with her right in front of me.

"I'm an asshole." He leaned away from me and lay flat on his back. "I'm sorry."

"It's okay," I said and lay flat on my back as well. We both just lay there, staring at the ceiling. I didn't know what to say now. I wanted to ask him what he really thought about me, if he'd ever thought about me in any other way. If he'd ever love me. But I knew that would be pathetic. Just like me. I hated feeling this way. He'd think I was crazy, acting all emotional over nothing.

"Doesn't it sometimes seem like the world is against you?" TJ finally said, his voice sounding different, less sure of himself.

"Yeah, it does," I agreed, wondering what he was talking about. "Why do you say that?"

"I just sometimes feel that way," he said, his voice even lower now. "Everything in my world has always been black and white. Hot or cold. Yes or no. But that's not always how life works. My life has always been me against the world."

"That's not true," I protested. "You have Cody, you have my family." I didn't want to tell him that he had me. That seemed too personal. Too revealing.

"Yeah, but in my heart and brain, it's all been me against the world." He sighed. "And I've always told myself that . . ." His voice trailed off and I waited for him to continue. However, after a few minutes of silence he still hadn't said anything and so I spoke up.

"You told yourself what?"

"Nothing, I'm not making sense." He rolled over and then I rolled over to look at him. His eyes were tender, but his lips were twisted. He looked so lost, like a little boy, and I felt myself loving him so much. My heart filled to the brim as I stared at him. I loved this man so much it hurt.

"You're so beautiful," he said softly, his eyes meeting mine.

"Thank you," I said in reply.

"It killed me to see you crying." He took a deep breath. "I thought something happened."

"Nothing happened."

"I know, but I thought . . ." His voice trailed off again and he closed his eyes. "This is a mess."

"What's a mess?" I reached over and touched his shoulder.

"Nothing." His lips twisted. "You're so special—you know that, right?"

"What's so special about me?" I joked, but my heart stood still as I waited for him.

"You just don't even know." His eyes seemed to darken and he was silent for a few seconds as he stared at me. "Oh, Mila, butterflies envy you." He reached over and caressed my face.

"Why would butterflies envy me?" I laughed awkwardly. The air seemed to stand still in the room as I waited for his answer.

"The sight of you. The sound of your laugh. The lightest touch of your arm. The smell of your hair. The way your eyes crinkle when you smile. The way you play with your hair when you're nervous. The way you listen to me. The way you make me feel when I'm with you. The whole world stands still when my eyes catch yours. The whole world stands still and even the butterflies are caught up in your aura."

"Oh, TJ," I said, about to say more, but he held a finger to my lips and smiled, a beautiful, handsome, heartwarming smile that made my heart ache. I reached over and pulled him closer to me.

"The sight of you ignites my heart, Mila. The sound of your laugh is music to my ears. Just knowing that I'm next to you, the way that makes me feel, it's enough to let me know . . ." His voice trailed off again and he looked away from me then.

"Let you know what?" I asked breathlessly.

"I knew I was falling for you when the world stood still," he said, as if he were talking to himself. He then looked back at me, a confused expression on his face. "When I saw you crying just now, it felt like the world was going to combust and burst into flames. It made me feel things. Think things." He sighed.

"Is that a good thing?" I asked him softly, hope starting to bubble inside of me.

"I'm still trying to decide." He looked confused.

"Do you love me?" I asked, my throat immediately freezing as soon as the words were out. How could I have asked him that? I wanted to die as soon as I'd said the words.

"I'm trying not to. I'm really trying not to." He looked so bleak and I wasn't sure, but I reached over to him to bring him even closer to me, to comfort him, even though it was my heart that was breaking. All I could think inside was *love me, love me, love me, please, love me.*

"Don't fall for me, Mila. Please don't fall for me," he said as he kissed my neck and held me close.

I already have. I closed my eyes and held him close, praying that more tears wouldn't start to fall.

Chapter Seven

TJ

Twenty Years Ago

THE WHOLE ROOM WAS DARK as I crawled out of bed. I was thirsty and hungry and I rubbed my eyes as I made my way to my bedroom door. I saw my toy soldiers on the floor next to my bed and picked up two of them to take with me to the kitchen. I walked quietly to the door, as I knew my dad would be upset if he knew I was out of bed. I'd get in trouble and grounded and I wouldn't be able to play video games, and that would suck.

My hand froze on the doorknob as I turned it and it squeaked. I paused and held my soldiers tightly as I peeked into the corridor. There was no noise and no doors were opening. I was safe.

I crept out of the room and walked softly, avoiding all the loose floorboards that I knew made noise. I made it to the top of the stairs when all of a sudden I heard a noise. I froze, my eyes widening, and I looked behind me to make sure my dad wasn't coming out. No doors opened, but once again I heard the noise. I tilted my head to the side and listened again. It sounded like a sob. As if someone were crying.

I felt my lower lip wobbling and I wasn't sure why. I started to head back to my bedroom but then stopped and walked towards the bedroom my mom slept in. My friends thought it was weird that my mom and dad slept in different rooms, but it was all I'd ever known.

I made my way to her bedroom and opened the door slowly. I stared into the room, my eyes adjusting to the darkness and then I saw her, curled up on the bed, her face in her hands and she was sobbing, her hair a mess on her pillow. I stood there, watching her, my heart thudding, my stomach feeling empty and my face turning red with heat. Her sobs seemed to get louder and louder as I stood there and I felt both of my toy soldiers falling to the floor. I bit down on my lower lip, scared that my mom heard the noise, but she didn't. If anything, her sobs got even louder. As her tears cascaded down her face I watched as her fists hit her pillow as if she were punching it. I didn't really understand what was going on.

"Mommy?" I said softly, not sure what to do. I wanted to go over and hug her. I wanted to go over and ask her if everything was OK. I wanted her to hold me in her arms and kiss the top of my head like she did every morning before I went to school.

But my feet wouldn't move. I leaned back into the doorway and started to suck my thumb. My dad would be pissed if he saw me sucking my thumb. He told me boys didn't suck their thumb. I tried not to, but there were some times when I just couldn't stop myself. This was one of those times. I wanted to be a big boy, I really did. I was eight, I should be able to stop, but sometimes I just couldn't.

"Mom," I said again, softly, wishing she would look up and see me, and stop crying, but she didn't hear me or see me. Instead she just kept crying and crying.

"I hate you. I hate you. I hate you," she cried out into her pillow and I started sucking on my thumb harder.

"Mom," I whispered, feeling scared, my whole body feeling cold with uncertainty.

"I just want to die," she cried out and I so badly wanted to go over to her and kiss her. I so badly wanted to go over to tell her I loved her. But I couldn't move. I couldn't get the words out of my mouth. I stood there for about ten more minutes and then quietly picked up my toy soldiers, closed the door and made my way to my room and crawled back into my bed, closed my eyes and pretended to sleep until sleep finally took me.

When I woke up the next morning, my father told me that my mother had gone to Heaven earlier that morning. All I did was stare at him as my heart closed in and my stomach tightened. He didn't reach out to hug me or ask me if I was okay and I didn't reach out to him. Instead I just walked back to my room, got back into my bed, curled into a ball and sucked my thumb.

Present Day

EVERY MORNING, I WOULD WAKE up and just lie there without opening my eyes. It used to be that I wanted to avoid the beginning of the new day for as long as possible. I'd lie there and imagine that I was somewhere else, anywhere else. Sometimes I'd picture I was on a deserted island somewhere, the sun on my face, the salty air caressing my cheeks as I tried to figure out how to climb the closest coconut tree and pick as many coconuts as I could. Other times, I would picture myself at Mila's house with her family, playing board games or just sitting around the dinner table talking about our days.

I'd always found it funny that they'd always seemed so interested in hearing about my life, as if I were important or mattered to them. No one else had ever seemed to care. Certainly not my father. He cared about: my grades, my sportsmanship and what girls I dated. There was nothing else in my life that was important to him. I'd learned at an early age not to bother going to him when I was happy, excited or sad. He didn't listen and he didn't care. And I learned not to care. Not about anything. It wasn't important. I wasn't important. Though for some reason I was important to Mila and Cody, and their parents, and even Nonno looked at me like I mattered. It was a strange feeling, nice, but uncomfortable.

When I woke up in the mornings now, I still kept my eyes closed, but it wasn't to think about other places I could be, it was to let my mind think about Mila completely unadulterated. I would picture her smile, the bright happy look in her eyes, the way she plays with her hair when she's nervous. I would think about the way she smells, like roses on a dewy day, fresh, crisp, clean, fragrant. I would imagine her touching my arm or chest, imagine her holding me close, pressing her head against my chest and holding me tightly. I would see myself pulling her into my arms and kissing her forehead and then we would just be there, bound together by some emotion I didn't want to acknowledge. And then as my anxiety crept in, and the doubts started to come, I would find my eyes opening slowly, ready to face the day, to forget the fantasy that I didn't think I really wanted. And then I would focus on the task at hand and on why there will never be a moment like that in my daydreams again.

This morning, I awoke, but I didn't just lie there. I didn't focus on anything. My eyes flew open and I looked over to the right to look at Mila, to see that she was okay. It was weird having her share my bed now. It was weird that sometimes I woke up and thought of her and kissed her and caressed her in my mind, yet in person—in real life—I just lay there, not able to express the feelings within, in person.

"Morning," I said softly when I saw her eyelashes fluttering as I faced her. I knew she was awake and was just trying to pretend she was sleeping. She didn't answer me and I smiled to myself as I felt a surge of happiness trailing through my body for no real reason. It always surprised me how happy I felt just being in her company. Unfortunately, I also felt surges of anger and jealousy when around her. If she looked at another guy and smiled in her sweet, friendly way, it enraged me. Didn't she realize that other men might read something into her smile? What annoyed me even more was wondering if she was interested in them as well? What really did she see in me? What did she want from me? Would she be happy to be with another man?

I knew these thoughts were irrational, but they always came and I absolutely hated them. I hated feeling like she was taking over my brain; making me think and feel things I didn't want to feel. She opened up doubts, pains, hurts I didn't want to think about. The happiness was a high, but the flipside of that, well, the flipside was dark.

"I said, good morning, Mila," I said again and reached over to tickler her under the arm.

"No, you didn't." Her eyes popped open as her body reacted and she pushed my hand away. "You said 'morning,' not good morning." She smiled at me sweetly as she yawned gently. I watched as she pushed her hair away from her face and wondered at how beautiful she was. How could her brown eyes do so much to me when she looked at me?

"So you were awake?" I grinned at her and leaned forward to give her a quick and soft kiss on the lips. Her eyes widened slightly and she just lay there and stared back at me as I moved back.

"I never said that." She bit her lower lip, her eyes sparkling. "My subconscious must have heard."

"Uh huh." I nodded, rolling my eyes. "That must be it."

"Yeah, it is." She laughed and then reached over and touched my hair gingerly, running her fingers through my unkempt, short, dark locks before leaving my hair and touching my face. Her fingers ran along my jawline, touching my stubble, touching me lightly as they made their way to my chin. Her fingers were dainty, light as she touched me, and I felt my body freezing uncomfortably. Her touch was like magic, but I didn't like it. I didn't like the way she looked at me adoringly as she caressed my face. It made me feel . . . well, I can't describe the emotion. It turned my stomach into knots and I felt like I couldn't breathe. I felt out of control.

"So are you feeling better this morning?" I asked her, pulling back and looking away from her. Sometimes gazing into her eyes was too unnerving for my equilibrium.

"Yeah, I suppose." Her voice was uncertain and I gazed at her again. This time it was her eyes that fell to the side uncertainly as she fiddled with her fingers. An awkward silence befell us and I stretched out in the bed and closed my eyes. I could feel Mila curling up and hugging herself next to me. I wanted to reach over and hold her tight. I wanted to tell her that we didn't have to be uncomfortable with each other. I wanted to hold her close and tell her to let her worries go. But I couldn't. Instead I pulled the sheet off of my body and turned to her with a wicked grin.

"Pleasure me, woman."

"What?" She gave me a funny look, her eyes narrowing as she looked down at my boxer shorts and then back to my eyes.

"I said, pleasure me, woman." I grinned at her as I joked, trying to break the awkward tension in the air. I wasn't really sure where it had emanated from, but I didn't like it. I was a lot more comfortable when the focus was on sex.

"Yeah, okay." Mila shook her head. "Give me a minute."

"I don't want to give you a minute." I grabbed her hands and pulled her towards me. "I want to feel those lips on my cock right now."

"You're so crude." She looked at me, annoyed, and my stomach flipped. "I'm not some toy or plaything, just here to pleasure you when you want."

"You're not?" I growled, my brain starting to feel panicked as I kept on joking.

"Touch me, woman."

"TJ." She shook her head, disappointment in her eyes, sadness in the tilt of her lips.

"Fine, don't," I said, laughing awkwardly, not really knowing what to say.

"Is this all I am to you?" she said softly, long drawn-out sighs leaving her mouth as her body moved away from me.

"No," I said abruptly, almost harshly. I sounded angry and that made me mad at myself. Why did I sound angry? And why was my stomach churning and my forehead heating up? I wanted to jump out of the bed. I wanted to go have a shower and a long run. I needed distance from her.

"All you want is sex." She looked disgusted and I wasn't sure if it was with me or herself.

"That's not all that I want."

"You don't want love and marriage, though, do you?" I could hear the hope in her voice. How could I tell her that in some sort of alternate reality, I wanted just that? In my deepest dreams I wanted that—the white-picket fence, the wife, three kids, a loud yappy dog and moody cat. But that was just a fantasy, not real life. My real life wouldn't go anything like that.

"You want a family and kids?" I asked, though I knew the answer.

"Yes," she said lightly. "Two boys, a girl. A Labrador Retriever."

"You'll have it," I said, though it killed me to say that. I didn't want to think of her with another man, married, giving birth to his kids. In fact it infuriated me. It made me want to kill the other man, even though he didn't really exist.

"I guess not in the next four weeks," she tried to joke, her words shaky.

"Yeah, not in the next four weeks." I smiled back at her, trying to forget that this arrangement was temporary. She wouldn't be here with me every morning. I didn't have to worry that she'd take over my life. She'd only be here for a few more weeks and then everything would be back to normal.

"So what exactly do you feel for me, TJ?" she asked again, and I froze. I didn't want to get into this conversation with her. After I'd seen her crying, I had wanted to punch something or someone. A part of me had been scared. I'd never seen her like that before. It had opened up something in me and I had let her into a part of my soul that had been closed off before.

"I don't know how to answer that question, Mila." I sighed, "I really don't."

"Do you love me?" she asked me again hopefully, and my heart lurched at her question. I didn't know why she kept torturing the both of us.

"I love you like family," I lied. I wasn't sure exactly what I felt for her, but I knew I didn't love her like a sister or anything like that.

"Like family?" I could see the hurt in her eyes and it made my heart thud a little harder. I wanted to reach out and touch her face, but I didn't. I couldn't. Some part of me, the part that was reserved, the part that was scared of emotions and feelings, didn't know how to reach out. I didn't know how to tell her the things I was feeling. I didn't even understand the things I was feeling. How could I tell her that the hurt in her face was the same hurt I felt beating in my heart right then?

"So you think of me as your sister?" This time her voice was angry, betrayed, and I swallowed hard.

"Obviously not, Mila. I wouldn't fuck my sister." My words were harsh, harsher than I'd intended, and I was annoyed at myself.

"Yeah, I guess you wouldn't fuck her, just everyone else," Mila said bitterly and looked away from me. I could feel that I was losing her and I was scared. I took a deep breath and reached out a hand to her arm. She flinched and pulled it away from me and I felt like she'd just slapped me in the face.

"Mila, I wish I could tell you what you want to hear. All those magical fairy-tale words that you deserve, but I'm no Prince Charming. I've never pretended to be." I rubbed my forehead. "I'm all sorts of messed up, and you know that."

"It's fine," she said softly, looking away. "I don't care. We don't have to talk about it. I'm fine."

I just lay there then, staring at her face as she avoided my eyes. I watched as her lips trembled and she started to play with her hair. I could tell that she was upset. She always fiddled with her hair when she was nervous or upset. I looked back up to her face and I could see that her eyelashes were moving quickly. My throat caught as I realized she was fighting tears. I'd done this to her. I felt over-whelmed and angry with myself. I didn't want to make her cry. I wanted her to be happy. I needed her to be happy. I was already in too deep. I knew she would end up hating me. I knew that the secrets I held would break her. I knew they would break her, but I couldn't help that.

I closed my eyes for a second and started talking. The words came slowly, since my brain wasn't functioning properly and I didn't know what to say.

"I do like you, Mila," I said into the silence, my eyes still closed. "I might even love you in some way. Some sort of love that grows from the heart like weeds in a garden."

"What?" she said, her voice timid, and I opened my eyes to look at her.

"My love for you is like weeds growing in a garden," I said, my voice bleak. "I don't want to love you, I'm trying everything I can to not love you, but the feeling keeps growing and getting stronger, no matter what I try to do."

"You don't want to love me?" She looked confused, her eyes wide, gazing at me with such an innocent expression that I felt a dagger cutting into my heart as I stared back at her. I didn't know how to explain it to her. I didn't even know how to explain it to myself.

"I'm not that guy, Mila," I said, my throat dry. "I don't want to lose myself in you."

"I don't think that could ever happen," she said, rolling her eyes as she continued to gaze at me. "You're frigging TJ Walker."

"TJ Walker, yup that's me," I said with a wry smile. "I'm King of the World."

"You have everything you could want: money, women, looks." She shrugged. "You've got the perfect life."

"My life is far from perfect and I don't think I've got it all."

"So what are you, then?" She sighed. "Are you broken?"

"You have to have been whole to be broken," I said, and Mila's eyes softened, gazing at me in compassion and, for a few seconds, understanding, as if she finally comprehended where I was coming from.

"Your parents really messed you up, huh?" She reached out and grabbed my hand.

"I guess." I shrugged. "I don't know." And I didn't. I guess a psychiatrist would have been able to tell me what was wrong. Where my fears of love and commitment came from. Maybe they could tell me why as much as my heart beat for Mila, she was the last thing I wanted in my life. I couldn't even tell her how I really felt. I couldn't tell her that I loved her as much as I hated her. I couldn't tell her that with every waking minute that I wanted to be with her, I wanted to forget her. I wanted to vanquish her from my life. How could I tell her that with every moment I loved her, I hated her. I hated her for making me feel like I wasn't in control. I hated her for being the sunshine in my life on a warm day and the storms in the clouds on a bad one.

I couldn't tell her because it would kill her. I knew it would kill her because it killed me. It killed me to know that I couldn't just express the feelings in my heart. I couldn't just go with the love. Oh how I wished I could go with the love. How I wished the other feelings of insecurity wouldn't pop up. How different would everything be if I could express the feelings in my soul? How different would it be if I understood the feelings in my soul? My jaw clenched as I realized that that was only one part of the equation, and there was so much more to our relationship now. We were digging ourselves into a deeper and deeper hole. A hole I wasn't sure we'd ever get out of. A hole that might lead to her never talking to me again. Oh, the pain of thinking that she'd never talk to me again. The pain of not having her in my life. It would kill me. It would turn me into a zombie. A dead person living on the earth, but with no real reason for living.

I couldn't change our path now, though. Everything was so complicated and fucked up. How could I start telling her the truth, after having told her so many lies? Would it even matter if I could tell her how much I loved her? What was my love, after all? What was the promise of a million dollars from a beggar? Or the promise of a fortnight of hot sun from an Eskimo? I had nothing to give that would make me worthy of her. Nothing to change our path of mutual destruction. I knew we were both going to be devastated at the end of everything. And it scared me more than I was willing to admit.

"Why are you like this, TJ?" She sighed. "I don't understand. Why does it have to be like this?"

"I don't know." I sighed too, squeezing her hands. I'd asked myself that question a million times and I didn't know. "Maybe this is just who I've always been."

"So we're just going to fool around for four weeks, while we stage a fake engagement, and then that's it?" she asked, questioning me, trying to withdraw her hands, but I wouldn't let her.

"Yeah, I guess so," I answered, not really sure what to say. She had no idea that the bomb that was coming was going to be much, much worse than that.

"It's so easy for you, isn't it?" She sighed. "Just jump in and out of bed with all the women you want and then just move on."

I shook my head. "It's not easy at all." She had no idea how unique she was, how special. How I couldn't even think of another woman in any way other than platonic. I'd lost all attraction to them. Which was ironic, as I'd always appreciated a nice ass and rack.

"So you were just born this way? Unfeeling? Uncaring?" she asked again, prodding. I didn't know what she was hoping to accomplish, and while I didn't want to see her hurting, I didn't know how to end the conversation to prevent that.

"I suppose so." I shrugged.

"Okay, then." She licked her lips and I could see the light in her eyes fading. "I understand." She nodded. "It's fine, really. We'll just have fun and then when it's done, we can just go back to being friends again." She looked into my eyes and gave me a big smile. "I'm an adult, I can handle it."

My heart broke then. The look in her eyes so proud, so determined, so heartbroken.

"I wish I could be the man you need me to be," I said, my voice lower than a whisper.

"What?" she asked me, leaning in closer.

"I'm glad you can be so mature about it," I said louder and her face froze as she nodded. My heart broke for her and it broke for me. I knew in that moment that both of our spirits were somehow fading, both of us forever connected to this moment. That hope and love had died slightly. That we were both victims to something we didn't understand. In that moment, I felt a piece of my soul being torn out of my body. I felt like ice was piling into my heart and stomach and I didn't know how to breathe.

It shouldn't feel this way. Yet, it did. I was doing this for her. I was doing this because I knew I couldn't give her what she needed. Not really. I didn't know how. And what was worse, I didn't know that all of me wanted to know how. As much as I loved being with her, I hated it. I hated how she made me feel. I hated the insecurity. I hated the jealousy. I hated the powerlessness. I hated that sometimes when I was alone and looking at the sky, her face would pop into my mind and I would find myself spending minutes and hours just thinking of her smile. I hated that I felt like she was made for me. She was my other half, my soul mate. She made me believe in God and that was a laugh because I hadn't believed in a long time.

"So, what do you want to do today?" I asked her finally, pretending that we hadn't just had the most life-altering conversation of our lives. I grinned at her, willing her to grin back. Willing her to go along with the façade that we were both cool with whatever this game was.

"I think I'm going to go and see Nonno," she said, attempting a smile. "Maybe go to the beach or something."

"Oh, that will be fun." I was annoyed that a part of me wanted her to ask me to go to the beach with them. I didn't really want to go to the beach; I just wanted to be with her.

"Yeah." She nodded. "It will be fun. Nonno will likely tell me more stories of him and Nonna when they were back in Italy." She laughed. "Shoot, he'll most probably tell the same stories to my kids and grandkids." She laughed and I just nodded, not wanting to go there. "I should get up and shower," she said feebly. I could tell that she wanted to be away from me, wanted to figure out her feelings, see what she was left with inside. I hoped I hadn't hurt her too badly. I didn't want to do that. I hadn't expected her to get so deep in conversation.

"Okay, that sounds good." I nodded and watched as she jumped out of bed. My body missed her as soon as she was gone. It was the first morning since she'd been here that we hadn't made love. I wanted to reach up and grab her and pull her back down onto the bed, but I didn't. She gave me a self-conscious smile as she walked away, her eyes looking small and sad, and I just grinned as she walked into the bathroom, pretending that I didn't notice her downtrodden spirit.

This was for the best. It was smart for me to get her to start hating me from now on. This way she wouldn't be so heartbroken and downtrodden when everything came out.

I heard the sound of the water in the shower and I felt tears coming to my eyes for the first time in years. I was a man who didn't cry. I was a man who didn't shed a tear, but in that moment I couldn't stop myself. I felt like I'd just lost a part of myself. I wasn't even sure how or why, but as the tears flowed, I knew that I needed the release. A part of me wondered if I was crying because she was crying in the shower. It wouldn't have surprised me. We were so connected. Our bodies attuned with each other's every action and feeling. I'd never experienced something so extrasensory before. I wouldn't have believed it was possible. Mila was my soul mate.

We were connected in ways I'd never have believed possible, but we were never going to get to be together for two reasons. One reason was the fact that she would hate me once she realized what I was hiding from her, and the second reason was because it confounded me to believe that she could love me and stay with me forever. I wasn't good enough for her. I wasn't the man she thought I was and I knew that it would kill me once she found that out and stopped loving me. I could lose everything in the world and not have it hurt as much as loving Mila and losing her when she realized who I really was.

Chapter Eight

Mila

THE GOAT AND THE FISH. That was us. He was the goat: frisky, moody, intelligent, questioning, hard to read. I was the fish swimming toward him, following him, wanting him, waiting for him. Always waiting for him. Every day I woke up and thought about how I wanted to kick that goat, though some days I didn't want to kick so hard. You don't kick hard when you love someone.

Every day felt different now. Some days, I could almost pretend that I felt happy, as if I were riding the bull of life and charging down the streets of Pamplona like some badass Spaniard with no fear. Those were the days I loved, feeling high on life, excited to just be me and to experience everything that I could. I craved all of the feelings that went through me: pain, happiness, joy, jealousy, love. All of them made me feel alive, like I had a purpose. And then there were the days that I didn't want to wake up. Even sitting up in bed was an effort. Thinking of him was a burden. A heartache. A depression. A memory I didn't want to relive.

Those days were always the same. The thoughts were always the same. The moment etched in my mind was always the same. We're at the lake. It's mid-September. It was a couple of years ago, when I was in college. I'd been so excited to go to the lake house that summer. Some part of me had thought that that was going to be the summer that TJ and I would finally get together. It was late that night, about eleven p.m. I remember the time exactly because he'd told me we had to be there by nine p.m. and I'd been late. We were scared we wouldn't see the constellation, but we still had hope. We were tired, but alert. He wanted to show me Capricornus, the sea-goat. I'd laughed. I'd never heard of a sea-goat constellation. He'd held my hand and told me to just wait. That there were several things I'd never heard of before. And so we lay back and waited. He told me how Capricornus was represented by an image of a hybrid goat and a fish. I joked that he was moody like a goat and he said I was antsy like a fish. I told him that I was on break from college, so I didn't need him acting like a bossy professor. He said I'd be so lucky. I'd just looked at him, confused, and asked him, "*lucky for him to be bossy?*" And he'd just laughed.

His shoulder had rubbed next to mine gently as we lay looking up at the stars, waiting. The distant stars and moon provided the only light and as I looked over at his shadowed face, I had felt my heart swelling. He looked over at me, gave me a small smile and told me to look back at the sky and to wait patiently. I remember I rolled my eyes at his bossy tone, but I didn't say anything. I liked it when he took charge. And then, just when I thought we were waiting in vain, we saw a shooting star and I felt his hand finding mine and squeezing. We just lay there, staring at the sky, hand-in-hand, and as the cool breeze ran across my face, I thought that this was perhaps one of the happiest moments I'd ever had in my life. I never wanted it to end.

"Do you believe in soul mates?" I had asked him softly, not able to stop myself.

"Soul mates?"

"You know, your one true love?"

"One true love?" He laughed, his eyes looking at me for a few seconds and then away from me. "I think there are many loves for everyone."

"I see." My heart dropped and I gave him my best fake smile and looked back at the sky.

"Why? Do you believe in soul mates?"

"I do," I said earnestly. "I believe that there's one perfect person made for everyone."

"Made by whom?" He laughed again.

"By God," I said stiffly, feeling awkward.

"Oh, okay." His voice trailed off. "Sure thing."

"Or, if you prefer, the universe. I think that there is one perfect person out there for everyone and when you meet them you just know."

"You just know what?"

"That they're the one, of course." I was starting to get annoyed. "You know that they are your true love. The one you've waited your whole life for. The one that just gets you. The one that your heart was made to love. In fact, they're already in your heart. And when you meet them, when you realize that they are the one, then you feel whole, as if everything in life makes sense."

"That's a nice fairy tale," he said with a laugh.

"I don't think it's a fairy tale."

"Well, good luck to you then, Mila. I hope you meet this perfect man, your soul mate, or whatever." His voice had been stiff and the air had gone silent.

That was the moment that I started to question everything. That was the moment I knew I loved him as more than a crush. That was the moment I knew that my fairy tale might never come true.

THERE'S A NUMBNESS IN PAIN that I welcome. It's a welcome change from gut-wrenching pain and emptiness that you feel when you love someone who doesn't love you. There is nothing worse than the feeling of rejection. There is nothing worse than not being good enough. There is nothing worse than the feeling in your heart when you realize that the man that you love doesn't love you back, even if you would have bet your soul on it that he did. I didn't trust my heart anymore, or my brain. They both lied to me. They told me that TJ loved me. I knew he didn't want to love me. I knew that he'd never told me he loved me, but something in me had still believed it to be true. Something in the way that he smiled, in the way that he looked at me, his possessiveness, that way he held me close, the way he talked to me. All of those things had told me he was the one. But it was all in my head. It was all a dream. A fantasy. I'd gone and made a fool of myself and I was embarrassed and ashamed and devastated. And my heart—well, I was surprised my heart was still functioning.

I'd left TJ's house that morning, anxious to get away from him and to see Nonno. Though a part of me had hoped that he would say, "Don't go. Spend the day with me, Mila," but of course he hadn't said those words. He hadn't said anything and I'd left and told him I'd see him later and he'd told me to enjoy my day with Nonno and to make it special. I'd smiled, but I hadn't been able to look him in the eyes. I hadn't wanted him to see the heartbreak in my irises.

I resisted the urge to check my phone again once I hit a stoplight. I knew that there wouldn't be any texts from TJ. I hadn't heard my phone beeping. He didn't care. He wasn't thinking of me as much as I was thinking of him. That didn't matter to me though. As soon as I was stopped, I grabbed my phone and quickly punched in my code to check my messages. My heart fell as I saw no new messages. It wasn't a shock, but just another confirmation that I was a sad case. This was the fifth time since I'd left TJ's home that I was checking my messages, praying and hoping for a sign that maybe—just maybe—he could love me back. But there was nothing. I continued driving to Nonno's house and I allowed myself five more minutes to cry before I was going to have to stop. I didn't want to show up to Nonno's house with a red nose and swollen eyes from all my tears.

I turned on the radio to see if I could cheer myself up with some music, when Adele's new single, "Hello", started playing. I sang along and felt the tears streaming once again. I wasn't sure why I allowed myself to listen to sad songs, when I was suffering from heartache. I knew it wasn't smart, but somehow it made me feel better. It made me remember that other people had gone through heartache as well and still ended up okay on the other side. My stomach felt empty as I sang along and drove. I wasn't sure that I was going to feel better once this was all over. I wasn't sure it was smart to even stay in this relationship with TJ. How could I keep giving myself to him? Sleeping with him? Loving him? Knowing that every moment with him made me love him more and made him feel like I was still nothing.

I turned onto the interstate and switched the radio off. I needed to dry my eyes and pretend to be happy for my meeting with Nonno. It always made him upset to see me hurting.

NONNO OPENED THE FRONT DOOR and pulled me into his arms. "Mila, so good to see you, mia cara."

"You too, Nonno." I kissed his cheek. "I'm sorry I haven't called or seen you in a while. I've just been preoccupied with TJ and the engagement."

"I understand." He smiled at me graciously as we walked into his home. I smiled as I saw that he had an old photo album out on the couch, and I walked over to it.

"Looking at photos of Nonna?" I asked him, smiling at how nostalgic he was.

"Every single day." He nodded and walked over to me and we sat down together on the couch and looked at the photos.

"She was so beautiful," I said as I picked up a photo of Nonna that must have been taken when she was eighteen. She was scowling at the camera, her long black hair flying behind her as she stood there with a basket in her hands. I laughed at the photo and Nonno took it from me and held it close to his eyes.

"This day, your Nonna, she was mad at me." He chuckled. "She was mad because she'd seen me talking to another girl. So when I came up to the camera, she told me to get away from her."

"Oh Nonno." I looked at him in surprise and smiled. "Were you flirting with the other girl?"

"Yes." He laughed. "I wanted to make her jealous." He looked over at me and winked. "She'd been talking to Alberto, the banker's son, the day before and I knew he had intentions to get to know her better. I needed to make sure she knew that she liked me."

"And so you flirted with someone else?" I said and shook my head.

"The games of love have been around for a long time, my dear." He laughed and put the photo back in the album carefully. We went through the pages and I stared at all the old photos of Nonno and Nonna as they'd gotten together. I stopped him from turning the page as I looked down and saw a photo I didn't remember seeing before. It was a photo of Nonno and Nonna and she was staring at the camera and he was staring at her. Even though it was only a photo, it was easy to see the love and devotion in his eyes as he gazed at her tenderly. And even Nonna was grinning into the camera softly, her eyes looking bright. There was magic in the photo, an air of love. It was clear to see and it made me shiver at the power of the shot.

"This is beautiful, Nonno," I said to him and he took the photo from me and held it tightly.

"She was beautiful," he almost whispered as he sat back. "My love, my amore," he said as he stared at the photo. "That day, the day this photo was taken, that was the day that I knew your Nonna and I would be together forever, that nothing would ever part us. That was the day I stopped worrying that she would meet someone else.

"Oh?" I asked him, my heart pounding. I was starting to feel emotional. I sat there wishing that TJ would feel that way about me, and that made me feel guilty. I didn't want to turn every situation into one where I was thinking about TJ.

"Your Nonna wrote me a poem. She read it to me right before that photo was taken," he said and looked at me, his eyes looking far away as he remembered the moment. "It was so unusual and I hadn't expected it. I was the romantic in the relationship and even then I was far from a Romeo." He smiled and then sighed.

"Do you remember the poem?" I asked softly.

"Do I remember?" He chuckled again. "It has been burned into my brain for decades," he said and looked back down at the photo. "It is one of my fondest memories."

"Tell me," I said and reached over and grabbed his hand. "Tell me, Nonno."

"Okay." He nodded and then he cleared his throat. He was about to start talking again when he had a coughing fit.

"Nonno, are you okay?" I asked as I watched him coughing. I felt helpless and wasn't sure what to do. I was about to start patting him on the back when he finally stopped coughing. "Nonno?" I asked again as I saw spots of blood on the tissue he had been coughing into.

"I'm fine." He shook his head and frowned. "Just a bad cough." He took a sip of water and then looked over at me and smiled. "Stop worrying and start listening."

"I am listening," I said and laughed.

"That moment when your heart skips a beat. When all worries turn to joy. When all fears fade away. That moment when our eyes meet. And our souls reconnect.

And the silence sings a song. That's the moment that I remember. That's the dance that I live for. That's the journey that I pray for. That's the you that I dream of. This is the moment I was made for." He stopped and I looked over at him, and saw tears running down his face.

"Oh, Nonno," I said and reached my arm around his shoulder. "I'm sorry."

"Don't be sorry." He shook his head and gazed into my eyes. "She was my true love and I miss her, but I will see her again."

"Oh, Nonno." I bit down on my lower lip. "You both had such a true love."

"There is nothing else in this world more precious than true love, Mila." His eyes were bright as he gazed at me. "There is nothing worth living for if you don't have love."

"Well, life itself, right?" I said, trying to make light of the situation.

"Life is for the living." He nodded. "And love is what makes life great."

"Yeah, I guess," I said as my heart lurched and I thought back to TJ again. "Some of us aren't as lucky as you and Nonna. Some of us don't have happy endings."

"What are you talking about, Mila?" His eyes narrowed as he looked at me.

"Nothing," I said and shook my head, embarrassed to tell Nonno exactly what was going on with me.

"Are you not happy, my Mila?" He studied my face shrewdly and I could feel the tears starting to build up. I didn't want him to know exactly what was going on. I knew that he had to know that something wasn't completely right. I mean, TJ had essentially just fallen into my pocket in a matter of seconds. Real life didn't work like that.

"I'm fine." I took a deep breath. I had to be a big girl. I was not going to let Nonno know how pathetic and sad I was.

"You want to go down to the beach?" Nonno jumped up, placing the photo album next to me.

"The beach?" I asked, flummoxed. "That's random."

"Let's go to the beach and talk." He looked at me lovingly. "We both could do with some fresh air."

"Oh." I looked up at him. He knew there was something I wasn't telling him. "Are you sure?"

"Yes, mia cara. You know you can't keep secrets from your Nonno."

"I know." I sighed and stood up. "I love you, Nonno."

"I know." He pulled me into a hug. "I love you more than anything, Mila. You're my beautiful princess and all I want is for you to be happy and taken care of."

"I know." I rested my head on his shoulder and looked up at him. "How did I get so lucky as to have you as my Nonno?"

"You're blessed." He kissed my forehead and grinned, his eyes sparkling before he started coughing again. He pulled back and grabbed his tissue, his expression changing to one of a frown.

"You sure you're okay to go out, Nonno?" I asked him, worried. "Sounds like you have a bit of a cold or something."

"I'm fine, my dear." He wiped his mouth. "Let me go and change into some warmer clothes and then we can leave."

"Okay." I nodded and watched as he walked out of the room. I then grabbed my phone from my pocket to see if TJ had called or texted. I was hoping he'd have left some sort of message saying something like, "I made a mistake, I really do love you, come home," but of course there was nothing there when I checked. My heart sank as I put my phone back into my pocket and I sat back on the couch and stared at the photos as I waited for Nonno to get ready.

THE BEACH WAS DESOLATE AS we walked along the sand. It was too cold for people to go into the water and there was only one guy on the beach with us and he was walking his dog. I stared at the dog as it ran down the beach chasing a branch and I thought to myself what a life the dog had as it ran back and forth to its owner, grinning with happiness. How simple life must be to a dog. What I wouldn't have given to have that sort of peace in my heart. It would make me feel like I had a purpose in life, as opposed to being a loser who could only focus on TJ and his not loving me.

"So, Mila, tell me what's going on." Nonno turned to me as we walked to the shoreline. "Tell me what's bothering you."

"Oh, Nonno, I feel like an idiot." I made a face, trying to sound lighthearted. I wanted to make a joke, but I felt like I was going to start crying. "I'm a fool. I could be a clown for a king or a court jester or something."

"Why do you say that, Mila?" Nonno frowned at me.

"Because I'm a royal fool. The biggest fool on the planet." I tried to smile at him, but he didn't smile back. Instead I watched Nonno's expression go from shrewd to sad and he stepped forward and grabbed my hands.

"You're not a fool, mia cara. Don't ever say that."

"I am." I sighed. I gulped and looked down.

"Then tell me, why are you a fool?"

"Because I really thought that there was a chance that TJ really loved me. I really thought that he could be the one for me."

"You don't think he loves you?" Nonno sighed. "And you love him?"

"I love him with all of my heart." I closed my eyes as my heart froze. "You don't even understand. It's something I feel in my soul. It's something that I can't stop thinking about. Just saying his name makes my heart jump for joy."

"I know the feeling. That's how I feel about your Nonna." He nodded. "That's true love, Mila."

"How can it be true love if he doesn't love me?" I sobbed. I knew Nonno was probably confused about why I was crying and why we would be engaged if we weren't in love, but I knew he was smart enough to know that obviously something was up. You didn't go from a lifelong crush to an engagement and deep love in 2.5 seconds.

"Mila, I'm going to need for you to explain to me exactly what's going on." Nonno grabbed my hands and turned me to face him. "I don't really understand what you're saying."

"I don't even understand what I'm saying sometimes." I took a deep breath. "And that's not the only thing, Nonno. I have a secret. Something I did years ago that he doesn't know about. And it's haunting me. Sometimes I think, what if he does fall in love with me and then he finds out what I did? Then he'll stop loving me."

"Mila, tell me what's in your heart." Nonno caressed my cheek. "I need you to tell me exactly what you're thinking. I need to know what's in your heart. What's in your soul. I can't help you if you don't tell me."

"I just don't know what to say. I don't know how to let you know what happened. I don't want you to be ashamed of me. I feel so weak." I sighed.

"I would never be ashamed of you, mia cara. You are my heart. You are my soul. Everything I do is for you. You're my only grand-daughter and you are everything to me. You know there is nothing I wouldn't do for you. All I want in this world is for you to be happy and to never suffer. It pains me to see you suffer. It pains me deep in my heart. Your pain is my pain. I don't want to see you cry. I don't want to see anything in your eyes that makes me think you're going through turmoil. You know that, right?"

"Oh Nonno, I know. I know how much you love me." I gave him a half-smile. "You're the reason I'm such a hopeless romantic." I laughed. "If it wasn't for all your and Nonna's stories, I wouldn't want to believe that true love existed. I wouldn't be such an idealist."

"So tell me what you're thinking."

"Sometimes I think he could love me," I said, my voice echoing all the hope in my heart. "Sometimes he looks at me with a light in his eyes that makes me feel like I'm the only person in the world, but then . . ." My voice trailed off as I looked out at the ocean and watched the waves crashing into the rocks, close to the pier. I felt too sad and too tired to continue. Even talking about the situation had the ability to make me feel empty inside.

"But then what?" Nonno asked me softly, his hand on my shoulder as we stood there.

"But then, I think I've imagined it," I said softly. "The moment disappears. The tenderness in his gaze, the lift in his lips, the knowing look in his eyes. It just fades. And then it's as if I'm looking into the soul of a stranger."

"You're being too dramatic, Mila," Nonno said and he sounded weary, as if he were attempting to take on the burden in my heart and put it on his shoulders.

"I'm not being dramatic." I turned to him. "I'm being realistic. I'm being safe. Nonno, when I look at him, my heart skips a beat and my stomach jumps. I feel happy. I feel excited. I feel like my soul mate is once again in my world. It's like every part of me knows that he is my other half. And every part of me wants him to know that I'm his other half too. Every part of me is craving for the moment he will suddenly realize who I am to him."

"Maybe he does know," Nonno said softly. "You can't rush these things. Maybe he's scared. You know he had a hard life with his dad after what happened to his mom."

"I know his dad is cold. I know his mom died when he was young. He never talks about it. I mean, can that still be affecting him?"

"Mila, of course that would still be affecting him. He's human. He was young when his mom died, remember that. Still a kid. These things have a way of staying with you for a long, long time. TJ's a good man."

"I know he's a good man." I sighed and bit down on my lower lip. "I know there's something inside of him that's broken. Sometimes I can see it in his eyes. Sometimes when I look at him, there's a sadness there, a sadness that makes me just want to reach out and hold him. Sometimes he looks at me like he has something he wants to say, something deep, and we just stare at each other and I wait to see what he's going to say, but then it's like his brain shuts down and he makes a joke."

"That's a preservation mechanism. He's probably not comfortable with expressing his feelings. He didn't grow up with a family like yours, Mila. You have to give him time. Reach him in ways that don't make him feel uncomfortable."

"I just want to know that he feels something. I just want to know that he knows that what we have is special. I want him to just give me one iota of what I'm giving him. I just want him to feel an ounce of the love for me that I feel for him. I want him to love me."

"And he will." Nonno grabbed my hands. "I know these things are hard, Mila, and I know that your patience is running thin, but he will come around."

"Not when he finds out." My voice was so soft that I wasn't even sure that Nonno could hear me. "Not when he finds out what I did. He may never forgive me then. Some secrets are just too much to overcome." My voice broke then and I fell to my knees as I watched the sun setting, signaling to me that another day had passed without me revealing the truth. Another day had passed and my heart was still in turmoil. I felt like I was on the downward spiral of some horrible rollercoaster ride. Nothing was going my way and while I just wanted to get off the ride, I wanted something epic to happen. I needed to feel the exhilaration of the anticipation of what was going to happen next, but it was just so hard. Too hard.

"What did you do, Mila?" Nonno came up from behind me and I stilled, ashamed to admit the lies that had sprung from my mouth. I knew that Nonno would be disappointed in me, as I was disappointed in myself.

"It's hard to admit." I sighed. "I was so immature, so jealous, but

I didn't really know what I was doing at the time."

"What did you do, Mila?"

"When Cody and TJ were in college, Sally and I went up for a weekend to stay with them in the apartment they were sharing. I think it was their senior year and Mom and Dad trusted them enough to show us around the campus. So anyway, it was a Saturday night and they left us in the apartment because they wanted to go to a frat party. They said we could just watch a movie, which is what we did. It was about ten p.m. Sally was on the phone with some pizza delivery place and there was a knock on the door." I took a deep breath, my face going red as I remembered that night vividly and I could feel myself heating up in shame.

"Continue," Nonno said, his eyes not leaving my face.

"So there was a knock on the door and there was this girl standing there." I spoke slowly, remembering the look on her face. She'd been worried and scared, her face pale as she stood there awkwardly. I'd known right away that something was wrong—call it female intuition or something. I looked at Nonno then and made a face, wanting to cry, but I knew that I'd made this mess by myself.

"Go on, mia cara."

"She asked for TJ." I chewed on my lower lip. "I asked her why. She started to cry so I told her to come in." I took a deep breath. "Nonno, she told me she was pregnant. She told me that there was a possibility that TJ was the dad and that she needed to talk to him. She asked me if she could wait for him."

"Okay." Nonno pursed his lips and stared at me, his expression not changing.

"I asked her how sure she was that TJ was the father. I asked her what she wanted. I told her that TJ and I were in a serious relationship. I told her that I wasn't sure we could handle the fact that she might be having his baby."

"Oh Mila."

"And then I told her to leave." Tears filled my eyes. "I told her she couldn't wait for TJ. I don't know why I did that, Nonno. I was so ashamed of myself. I don't know what I was thinking. I was so jealous, I wasn't thinking properly. And she just left. She didn't even say anything. She wasn't even a bad person. She wasn't one of those bitchy money-grubbing girls that I hate. She wasn't super beautiful or slutty or anything. There was nothing about her that would make me think that I needed to protect TJ. Nothing predator-ish about her. I mean, she was even honest that TJ might not even be the father."

"So she just left?"

"Yes." I nodded.

"And I'm assuming you never told TJ."

"Nope." I shook my head. "When he got home that night, I was still too embarrassed, and selfishly I was hoping that he'd notice me, tell me he wanted to be with me or something."

"Oh Mila." Nonno sighed.

"I know," I said. "And then the next day, I was so embarrassed and ashamed of myself. I didn't know how to bring it up. I mean, I tried several times, but it just didn't seem right. There was never a perfect moment. I didn't want him to think badly of me, Nonno. And then, well then I figured the girl would most probably contact TJ and let him know. The next few weeks I waited for TJ to contact me all angry and tell me how pissed he was at me for talking to the girl and sending her away. But he never did. And then I forgot it. I tried to tell myself that it was likely that TJ wasn't the father and that the girl had figured out who it was." I rubbed my eyes. "But who knows, maybe she was just trying to help me and my fake relationship."

"You need to tell him, Mila. Nothing can continue, good or bad, if you're not honest with him."

"I'm scared to tell him." My eyes widened.

"You can't live your life being scared, Mila. You have to take chances, you have to grab the bull by the horn and go for it."

"I'm scared the bull is going to buck and rear and I'm going to fall off and get bruised."

"That's the risk you take in life and love, Mila."

"I just feel like this secret is so big that even if there was a possibility of him loving me that it would all fade away now. Who can forgive someone for something like that?"

"Everyone has a secret, Mila."

"But are all secrets forgivable?" I sighed. "I mean, I think a part of him could really love me. I just feel it in my soul. But I don't want to push for it, when this is still hanging over me. I need to know that if he does fall in love with me, it's for everything that he knows about me; good and bad."

"Just as you love him for everything you do and don't know, right?" Nonno said. "Good and bad."

"There is no bad in TJ." I sighed. "He's perfect."

"No one's perfect, Mila. We all have our secrets. Remember that."

"You don't have any secrets, Nonno. You're perfect too."

"Even I have secrets, Mila." He touched the top of my head. "Even I have secrets, but that doesn't mean that I love you any less."

Chapter Nine

TJ

Ten Years Ago

IT HAD BEEN TEN YEARS since my mother's death and I was leaving for college the next day. I figured I might as well ask my dad what had happened that night. I wanted to know. I wanted to understand. I wanted to somehow reach the parts of me that had been locked off my whole life. I didn't like being the cold, uncaring guy. I wasn't that guy. I had so many feelings inside, but I didn't know how to express them or get them out. I didn't know how to be open. And the older I got the more uncomfortable I was about love and relationships and getting too close. I'd dated some girls that had balled their eyes out when we'd broken up. They'd cried and told me they hated me and loved me and wanted to die and it scared me. I didn't want to make anyone feel like they weren't enough just because they weren't what I wanted. I mean, if I was honest with myself I didn't want to get emotionally involved, period. That was not who I was or who I would ever be. I'd never been in love. Never even thought I was close, and was glad for it. I didn't want that power over anyone and I didn't want anyone to have any power over me.

"Dude, what are you doing?" Cody hit me in the shoulder. "Let's go."

"Hold on, I need to ask my dad something first."

"Hurry up. The guys are waiting." Cody frowned and looked at his watch. I knew he didn't care about the waiting guys as much as he cared that Lisa, the head cheerleader, was into him and also waiting at the bowling alley for us.

"Dude, chill. I'll be back to talk in a few minutes," I said and left him in my bedroom and headed towards my dad's study. I knocked on the door and waited for him to let me come in.

"Dad," I said as I opened the door and walked in. He was sitting at his table, drinking a glass of what I supposed was whiskey or gin and staring at a contract.

"What's going on, TJ?" He looked up at me and then back down at the contract.

"Can we talk?" I asked him as I walked over to the desk.

"I'm going over a contract." He frowned. "Can we talk later?"

"No." I shook my head. "I want to talk now."

"I'm really quite busy." He took a sip of the warm brown liquid in his crystal glass.

"This won't take long," I said and placed my fists on the table in front of him and leaned into his face. "I want to talk now."

"What do you want to talk about?" He put his glass back on the table and then gazed at me, his face void of expression.

"I want to know about the day Mom died," I said and waited for him to react, though he didn't even blink.

"Okay." He shrugged. "What do you want to know?"

"What happened that day? Why was she so upset? Why did she take those pills?"

"Your mother had issues. Suffered from depression. Who knows why she did what she did."

"That's not a good answer, Dad." My eyes narrowed and I looked at him coldly. "Why did she hate you? Why was she crying? Why didn't you seem to care when she died?"

"I loved your mother, TJ." He leaned back and picked up his glass again slowly and took a long sip. "She had her issues. I got tired of having to deal with them. I referred her to shrinks. She was on medication. I did everything I could do, but she didn't get better. That's not my fault."

"What issues did she have?" I banged the table. "Give me something, goddammit. I need something concrete."

"Your mother was mentally imbalanced." He shrugged again. "Maybe she just had a few screws loose. You should be glad you don't have that same issue."

"Don't say that." I stood tall. "You're an uncaring, unfeeling asshole. You drove her to that, didn't you?"

"Drove her to what?" My father sighed and leaned forward again. "Why are you so emotional, TJ? That's a trait you get from her. You can't let emotions screw with your head in business. Emotions make everything gray. You need to deal with the black and white. You don't think your mother's death hurt me? You don't think I wondered every single day what I could have done to make it so she didn't kill herself? You don't think I would have done anything I could have to have stopped it? But she wasn't rational. She was always in her head. Overthinking things. Overthinking life. Overthinking everything I said and did. Every little thing I said. Everywhere I went. She had issues. She wanted to know where I was at all times. Who I was talking to. She was jealous. She was emotional. She loved me too much. She loved with her head in the clouds. All she thought about was love and me. I was her life. It was too much. I had a business to run. I couldn't be her life. I couldn't be her reason for being. She lived for me. I lived to make money. It wasn't a good match. I didn't realize that at first. Not until it was too late. I couldn't deal with it. I couldn't deal with her. I had other women, yes, and that killed her."

"So you cheated on her?"

"It wasn't personal." He shrugged. "I still loved her. I was still married to her. She was my wife. She was the mother of my child. I built this empire for you. And for her. She had it all."

"She had it all, but your love."

127

HELEN COOPER & J. S. COOPER

"Son, I'm going to give you some advice today that I wish every-one gave their child. Love is a construct. Love is something that people put in their heads to make themselves feel better about their lives. Live your life without love; it will make you feel a lot better. It will make you a man. You'll appreciate everything that much more. Trust me. Don't bother with love. Don't fall in love and don't let anyone fall in love with you. It's for the best. All love does is ruin lives. Either your life or another. If there's one thing you ever take from me, it should be that. Don't ever let love ruin your life or someone else's. That's what killed your mother. Love. Love ruins everything.

"That's all you have to say?" I stared at him for a few seconds and I watched as he took another sip of his whiskey and looked back at his contract. I stood up slowly and walked out of the office. "I'm ready," I said to Cody as I walked back into my bedroom.

"Finally," he said and jumped up with a grin.

"Yeah, finally," I said and gave him a small smile, my heart feel-ing worse than it ever had before.

Present Day

THERE'S THIS DREAM THAT I have. This dream of one day being able to say exactly what I'm thinking, exactly what I'm feeling, exactly what I'm wanting. There's a burning hope inside of me that one day the words will come easier, the fear will be less intense, and the deep yearning will not feel like it's attached to my very essence. I want to tell her one thing. I want to tell her I love her. I want to tell her that I think of her every morning and night. I want to tell her that I can't get her out of my mind. I can't sleep. I can't stop the racing of my heart when she smiles at me. I can't stop myself from smiling in response. I wish her every smile was for me. I want to capture them in a jar and release them every time I feel down. I want her to know that she makes me feel things I don't know that I want to feel. I'm not sure how to tell her I'm not good enough. I don't know how to tell her that I don't know that my love is enough. I don't know how to tell her that with every beat of her heart I feel life inside of me. I don't know how to tell her she's my soul mate. So I don't. I just watch her and wait. Wait to see what'll happen. Wait to see if she can read my mind. Wait to see if the feelings will go. I hope the feelings will go. I don't do love. Not like this. Not when I feel like I can't breathe. So this dream, this dream that keeps me up at night—it's all I have. It's all I need. And every day, I feel myself losing her just a little bit more. And every day I feel myself loving her just a little bit more. If she could read my mind, she'd know. She'd know that she's it for me. I just don't know if I can ever be it for her.

"So what's up?" I asked Cody as he sat in my office.

"You know what's up." He glared at me.

"Not really? The sky? The sun? The clouds?" I asked him and looked at my watch to indicate that time was running and I had work to do.

"This thing with Mila. I don't really know what's going on, but I know that there's something going on." He stood up and started pacing. "What game are you playing, TJ?"

"You know I have feelings for Mila," I said stiffly.

"I know that this engagement isn't really real," Cody said, his voice getting angrier. "Nonno called me last night. He's not sure exactly what's going on, but he's concerned. He asked me to look out for Mila."

"I don't know what to say, Cody." I shrugged and looked away from him. How could I explain to him what was going on? I couldn't tell him the truth. I wondered if this whole thing would cost me the best friend I'd ever had as well.

"You need to stop playing with her feelings, TJ." Cody's face was angry. "This isn't just a crush for Mila. She loves you."

"She doesn't know what love is." I grit my teeth as I stare at him. "She knows the score."

"You're my best friend, dude, but I swear to God . . ." Cody's face grew redder and I could see his fists were clenched.

"What?" I stood up and moved closer to him. "You want to hit me?"

"Yes." He scowled and looked up into my face. "I want to hit you." He took a step back and sighed. "But I'm not a hypocrite."

"What are you talking about?" I frowned, as I realized that not only was he angry with me, but he was angry with himself as well.

"I haven't exactly treated Sally well." He shrugged. "Maybe we both just suck."

"Are you saying I haven't treated Mila well?" I asked, but I knew the answer.

"I'm saying you haven't treated yourself or Mila well." His eyes pierced mine and I felt my heart stop. This was the first time Cody and I had ever really had a serious conversation about relationships. "If you love her, you're not doing yourself any favors."

"You know I don't do love. You don't do love either," I said weakly, a weird feeling entering my stomach. "It's just who we are."

"Yeah, but what I don't know is why." He shook his head. "I'm tired of fucking around. I want something real."

"Well, you always have Sally."

"I'm not fucking good enough for Sally." His face twisted. "She deserves someone better than me."

"Yeah, she does." I nodded and thought of Mila's best friend and how long she had pined for Cody. I pictured the looks of disappointment and pain on her face every time Cody did something that hurt her. "But that doesn't mean you can't be the man she deserves." I looked into his eyes seriously. "You can be that man."

"Are you going to be that man for Mila?"

"I don't know if I can." I shrugged and closed my eyes. My throat felt constricted and my head felt heavy as I thought about her.

"You're a fool." Cody shook his head at me. "You're going to lose her and you're going to wake up one of these days and you're going to wonder what happened."

"This engagement is complicated."

"What relationship isn't complicated?"

"This isn't a normal relationship."

"TJ, you're my best friend. I trust you, man. I trust you with my life. But this is my sister. I know I don't know what's going on here. I know that you don't seem to want to tell me, but I gotta ask you this, what you're doing here, can you promise me that you're doing it with good intentions?"

"Yes." I nodded. "I can promise you that."

"Okay." He sighed and I could see him thinking. "God, I hope you know what you're doing."

"I'm not sure that I really do," I said under my breath, but he didn't hear me.

"I know you're busy, so I'm going to go now," Cody said. "Maybe I'll give Sally a call to see how she's doing."

"You sure that's smart?" I asked him.

"Are either of us doing what we think is smart?" he asked me with a raised eyebrow and I just stared at him as he left the office. He was right. I knew without a doubt in my mind that neither of us were doing something smart. I let out a huge sigh as I looked at the paperwork on my desk. My dad had left a contract on my desk that was going to completely change the face of Mila's parents' company; something they were vehemently opposed to. However, because Mila had a fifty-one percent stake in the company, thanks to Nonno, she could make all final decisions. Which meant that I had that power now, legally, thanks to the papers we'd signed. I jumped up, grabbed the papers, put them in my briefcase and decided to leave the office. I couldn't do this now. Not while I was in this inner turmoil. Even though I knew eventually I was going to have to go behind Mila's back, had in fact already gone behind Mila's back, I just couldn't do this now. Not when I knew she'd gone crying to Nonno about me. Not when Cody was watching my every move. Everyone was going to be blindsided and there was nothing I could do about it. I wasn't ready for that move yet. I needed to go and see Mila. I needed to let her know that I was trying my best, and while I knew that would never be enough and wouldn't be enough to stop the betrayal, it would have to do for now.

I CALLED MILA AS SOON as I got to my car. "Hey, can you get out of work early today?" I sat in the driver's seat, my keys in the ignition, waiting, before I drove off.

"Not sure, why?" she asked curiously. "Is there another business meeting that you need me to attend?"

"No." Kinda.

"Oh okay? Any more information would be nice." She laughed and I smiled in response.

"I thought we could do something. Just the two of us," I said softly. "Let me apologize for overreacting in the restaurant last week."

"You don't have to do that," she said softly. "We all do things we regret sometimes. I already forgive you."

"Thank you," I said, my heart swelling. Mila really was too good for me. "But does that mean that you don't want to play hooky with me today?"

"What does playing hooky with you mean exactly?" she asked, teasing me, and I felt my loins stirring. She knew me all too well.

"It means we're going to have some fun."

"Up on a roof sort of fun?" she whispered.

"Would that be so bad?" My heart thudded.

"No," she said lightly and my heart soared.

"So play hooky with me?"

"Shouldn't you be working, TJ?" She giggled. "I know I should be working. Stuff around here isn't good." She sighed. "I'm worried."

"Why?" I asked softly, though I already knew her family business was in trouble.

"My parents are arguing all the time and I know we've lost a lot of revenue." She spoke quietly. "I'm not sure what's going to happen. I really shouldn't leave early."

"We can talk about, it if you want," I said, my heart going out for her. "And are you really working hard right now or are you goofing off and texting with Sally?"

"We only sent a few texts." She giggled.

"A few hundred?"

"Something like that," she admitted. "Okay, fine. Where are we going?"

"It's a surprise," I said happily. "Meet me at home in thirty minutes."

"Yes, sir," she said and I knew she was rolling her eyes at my bossy tone.

"Good girl." I chuckled and then I hung up before she could reply.

"SO WHERE ARE WE GOING?" Mila asked me eagerly as she sat in my front seat and stretched her arms out.

"It's a surprise. How many times do I have to tell you that?"

"Until you tell me where we're going."

"It's not going to happen," I said and looked over at her. "How are you feeling?" I said, my voice quieter as I gazed at her, trying to figure out how she was feeling inside. There was so much going on between us and at her work. I knew her happy exterior was just a facade, especially considering what Cody had told me about her visit with Nonno. I knew I was going to have to talk to Nonno. He was bound to have questions. I wasn't sure what I was going to say. Everything was turning out to be so much more complicated than I'd ever thought it was going to be.

"I'm okay." She shrugged and gave me a small smile. "Why?"

"I know you're upset with me," I said honestly. "I know this is a lot more complicated than we both thought it was going to be when we talked about this fake engagement."

"It's fine." Her eyes looked away from mine. "It's fun, right? I mean, let's just concentrate on that."

"This isn't about fun," I said seriously. "I hope you understand that, Mila."

"I do." She nodded. "Let's just enjoy the day. We don't need to have a serious talk." She looked at me with the sweetest smile I'd ever seen and my heart dropped as I realized just how much she meant to me.

"I don't want to hurt you," I started and she reached over and grabbed my arm.

"TJ, it's fine. We're fine. I spoke to Nonno yesterday and I'm feeling better. We just need to be ourselves and what's going to happen will happen."

"What does that mean?" I frowned.

"It just means we can't force anything." Her voice sounded wistful. "And, well, I don't wanna be the person who tries to force something that isn't there. I don't want to be that girl."

"What girl?" My hands gripped the steering wheel.

"It doesn't matter." She sighed. "I don't want to talk about it."

"Mila," I said softly as I headed onto the highway, "we're going to talk about it."

"I don't want to," she said, almost pouting.

"Mila." I glanced at her. "Talk to me. Please."

"Let's just say, I've spent too many years thinking with feelings and emotions and I don't want to be that person anymore." She looked out of the window. "I've made mistakes in the past. I've said things. Done things. And now I look back and think, what was the point? What did it get me?"

"Are you talking about another guy again?" I said, jealousy stirring in the pit of my stomach. "Is there some guy you regret being with?"

"It's not that." She sighed again and I knew I was being ridiculous, but I couldn't stop myself. "I just don't want to be the girl floating around with her head in the clouds anymore. I don't want to be the girl who's dreaming of rainbows and butterflies on a day that's thunder-storming."

"What girl do you want to be?"

"I want to be the girl who dances in the rain. I want to be the girl who jumps in puddles. I want to be the girl who can stare at the gray sky and watch the lightning and know it's okay to appreciate the darkness. I don't want to be the girl who can only survive in the sunshine. Life's not all sunshine. I don't want to pretend that it is anymore."

"I want your life to be all sunshine," I said before I could stop myself.

"I know you do." She nodded. "You care for me. I know that."

"But?" I said, glancing at her.

"But nothing." She rubbed the temples on her forehead. "When you live in the clouds, sometimes you just have to come back to earth every once in a while."

"I see," I said and my stomach sank. What was she saying? Did she no longer love me? Did she no longer want to be with me? Did she no longer care what I thought? Was she giving up on me? As much as that should have made me feel better, it didn't. It felt like a dagger through my gut.

"Let's just enjoy our day together," she said simply. "Let's enjoy our four weeks together and then when it's over we can go back to being friends. Maybe we'll even be best friends now."

"That's what you want?" I said, my stomach tightening. "To be best friends?"

"Sure. You're a great guy. I think maybe we've been destined to be best friends."

"Even though you have Sally and I have Cody?"

"They're still our best friends, but we have another kind of best friendship," she said and then sighed. "You know what I mean? Maybe we're soul mates, but on a different level."

"Yeah, maybe," I said and then turned the radio on. I didn't know what to say. I didn't know if she was saying this stuff because she really believed it or because I'd broken her. Maybe she didn't want to waste her time loving someone who couldn't love her back. She didn't say anything else after that and neither did I. I wasn't really sure what to say. She already knew what I thought about soul mates and one true love. I didn't believe in it. And she knew that. I thought there were multiple people out there for everyone. You just had to make it work, if a serious relationship was something that you really wanted. I knew she hated that. I knew she wanted to believe in a fairy tale. I didn't think it was safe or healthy. I think it set people up for devastation and despair. How could there only be one person? How could one person mean so much to one person? It wasn't good. What if it didn't work out? What if one person fell out of love? It would be too hard. Someone might not be able to take it. Someone might kill themselves. No, it was unrealistic and too scary a prospect to think that there was only one true love for everyone. Though, that didn't stop an inner hope in me that she thought I was her one. I nearly slammed on the brakes as I realized that. I wanted Mila to think I was her soul mate. I wanted her to think I was her one. Even though I didn't believe in it myself. I knew it was selfish of me. I knew I could never be that man in her life, yet I couldn't make that feeling go away. I was a horrible, selfish person. An absolutely horrible person.

"We're here," I said as we pulled up outside the stables.

"We're going riding?" She looked surprised as she undid her seatbelt. "That wasn't what I expected."

"What were you expecting?" I grinned at her.

"Aw, you'll never know." She winked at me and jumped out of the car and slammed the door. I jumped out and locked the doors and hurried over to her.

"Tell me." I grinned, wondering exactly what she thought we'd be doing and where.

"Nope." She grinned back at me.

"Come on, maybe you'll give me a good idea."

"Maybe you don't need any more good ideas." She laughed. "Now take me riding or I will pout."

"I don't want you pouting." I grabbed her hand. "Come on, then." And I guided her towards the office, where I knew they were waiting for me with two chestnut mares.

"So how come you took today off?" Mila asked me as we walked towards the stables. "I thought you were a dedicated employee?"

"Sometimes we all need a break, right?" I answered casually, ignoring the feeling in my gut that told me to tell her exactly what was going on.

"You can say that again." She sighed loudly. "I just don't know what's going to happen. We're bleeding money. Nothing is going right and Mom and Dad can't agree on the next step and they don't want to go to Nonno for advice."

"Why not?" I asked hesitantly. "He ran the business successfully for years, so why wouldn't they ask him for his advice?"

"I guess maybe pride? Or they're ashamed. Like, I think Nonno knows the economy is bad right now, but I don't know if he knows just how badly we're doing." She chewed on her lower lip. "I wanted to mention it to him, but I thought it would be too much."

"Why would it be too much?" I asked her, studying the side of her face as she played with her hair.

"Well, I didn't want to inundate him with all my problems."

"All your problems?" I raised an eyebrow at her. "How many do you have?"

"A few." She laughed. "Just a few."

"Am I one of the problems?" I asked dumbly, knowing the answer already.

"Could you ever be a problem, TJ?" she teased me and I laughed.

"Nope, never. I could never be a problem." I laughed as well and we entered the office. There was a young girl sitting behind the desk who was wearing a riding hat and I walked over to her. "Hi, I'm TJ Walker. I booked two horses for an afternoon ride."

"Oh, hi, Mr. Walker." She jumped up and grinned. "We got the two mares ready for you. We'll just get you some hats and crops. You guys have been riding before, right?"

"Yup." I nodded and looked over at Mila, who was grinning in excitement. "You look happy."

"I love riding." She nodded at me, but of course I already knew that. That was why I'd planned the afternoon adventure. "This is so cool. Thank you."

"No, thank yous needed. I wanted us to have a good time. Time for just us. That isn't about work, or the agreement."

"Or me going on and on about love." She laughed and then blushed.

"Let's just have a good afternoon." I reached over and squeezed her hand and she nodded. I wasn't sure what I was doing. A part of me felt guilty, like I was leading Mila on, in a way. I wanted to make it clear to her that this was never going to result in the true love that she wanted, but I was too selfish to just let her go completely. If I was a good guy, I'd stop sleeping with her and I'd just treat her as a friend, but I guess I wasn't a good guy. I craved her and I wasn't about to stop my addiction just yet.

"I'm down for that." She nodded and her eyes glazed over for a few seconds, before she started smiling again. "Let's go gallop."

"I'm down for that." I winked at her and she burst out laughing.

"You're incorrigible, TJ. I swear, you really are."

"That's what they all say," I said and she stuck her tongue out at me. I grabbed her around the waist and then pulled her towards me and gave her a big kiss. "But you're the only one I care about that says it to me," I whispered against her lips and I watched as her eyes lit up happily.

"I'M OUT OF BREATH," MILA said as we got off of the horses to take a break from riding. "This is a really beautiful setting," she said as she looked around the lush green field. "I can't believe I've never been here before."

"I know. I can't believe you've never been here before either." I smiled at her as she bent down to smell some wildflowers.

"This has been really fun," Mila said, her eyes bright and her face flushed as she looked up at me. "Should we head back to the stables now? It's going to be dark soon."

"No, I think we'll be okay," I said and grabbed the bag the girl had given me before we rode off. "We'll let the horses roam for a bit while we sit."

"Sit?" she asked me, surprised.

"We'll sit and eat."

"What are we eating?" She looked down at the flowers again and then at me and I laughed.

"No, Mila. I have a picnic."

"You have a picnic?" She looked at me with a shocked expression. "Where?"

"In my pants."

"TJ!"

"I'm joking." I winked at her and opened the bag that the girl had given me. "Let's sit." I sat down on the grass and Mila sat down next to me. I took out two turkey club sandwiches, a bag of chips, some chocolate chip cookies and grapes. "I'm afraid I don't have any wine or champagne, but I do have plenty of water."

"Wow, this is amazing. And so thoughtful." She looked at me with a curious expression. "I have to admit I'm surprised."

"Why? You didn't think I could be romantic?"

"I—I don't really know." She shrugged. "I'm touched you did this for me."

"I'm a nice guy, underneath it all." I smiled at her and handed her a sandwich. "I know that might be hard to believe, but I am a nice guy."

"I never thought you were a bad guy."

"That's good." I opened the bag of chips and then passed it to her. "Salt and vinegar, I hope that's okay."

"You know I love salt and vinegar." She grinned and grabbed a handful. "You're just being modest now."

"Who me?" I laughed and watched as she eagerly ate some chips.

"Yes, you." She took a bite of her sandwich and I just watched her eating as we sat there. "Aren't you hungry?" She made a face at me as she chewed. "You're just staring at me weirdly."

"That's because you have a weird face."

"You have a weird face." She glared at me.

"Not as weird as yours." I wiggled my eyebrows at her. "Are you from Mars?"

"No, I'm from Uranus." She giggled.

"You're from my anus?" I teased her. "Nice to meet you, part of my body."

"You're so gross, TJ Walker." She leaned over and hit me in the shoulder and I grabbed her arm and pulled it up so I could tickle her. "TJ." She squealed. "Stop, stop."

"Stop or what?" I laughed as I pinned her down to the ground. Her eyes were dancing as she pushed against me.

"I'll kick you in the nuts." She giggled as she wiggled against me.

"I'd like to see you try." I winked at her, and leaned my chest down on her lightly. "I don't think you'd do it," I said as I kissed her lightly.

"Oh really?" she said breathlessly, kissing me back lightly.

"Really," I said as I kissed the side of her face and ran my hands through her hair. She reached up and ran her hands down my back and I let my chest crush against her breasts. We rolled over onto our sides and our legs entwined together.

"Really," she said, her eyes fluttering open as she pulled back slightly. "I can do it now and prove it to you."

"Do what?" I growled at her as my hand crawled up to her breast and squeezed.

"You know what." She moaned as I pinched her nipple lightly and I could feel her nails digging into my arms.

"You can do that, but if you do, I won't be able to do this," I said and pushed my hardness into her belly. I could feel her body shaking as I held her and I slipped my other hand under her top and under her bra.

"TJ, don't." She tried to push my hand away. "Someone might see."

"Who?" I raised an eyebrow at her. "The horses?" I leaned over and sucked on her neck. "I don't think they care."

"Oh, TJ," she moaned and I felt her hand reaching down to my hardness and squeezing. I grinned as I felt her pressing her breast against the palm of my hand.

"Yes, dear Mila?" I asked as I pulled her top off and then undid her bra.

"Don't stop," she whispered as I bent down and took her nipple in my mouth. "Just don't stop." She purred as I nibbled on her breast lightly and I growled against her while I felt myself growing even harder.

Chapter Ten

Mila

"SO YOU GUYS HAD FUN horseback riding, huh?" Sally asked with narrowed eyes as she gazed at me.

"Yes, he just wanted to surprise me and clear the air," I said as I looked around TJ's apartment to make sure it was clean and presentable for our first dinner party. "It was amazing."

"Clear the air?" Sally cocked her head. "You mean because you're in love with him and he's an ass?"

"No." I shook my head at her and sighed. "It's been intense between us and maybe I've been pushing it too much. TJ never made any promises to me. I like him. He likes me. We're having fun and I'm helping him with a business deal. That's it."

"You're having kinky sex with him and you love him. That's just a little bit more complicated than what you just said." Sally put her hands on her hips and her lips thinned. "I don't want you to get hurt."

"I'm fine."

"You're not fine." She sighed. "We both know that. But you're telling yourself you're fine because you want to be with him."

"Sally, not tonight, please."

"Fine." She shrugged. "Not tonight. Tonight we will have fun, but it's something you need to think about seriously. The more you give of yourself, the more it's going to hurt at the end."

"So you're not even pretending that you think there's going to be a good ending for me now?"

"What do I know?" She sighed again and gave me a weak smile. "I'm just worried for you. You know what they say about guys. Take them at their word. If he says he doesn't love you and he doesn't want a serious relationship, well, that's what he means."

"Yeah," I said and looked away from her, my heart pounding and my head starting to feel sad again.

"Ignore me." She grabbed my hands and gave me a huge smile. "I'm just bitter because Cody doesn't have the time of day for me."

"Didn't he call you last week?"

"Yeah, it was just some random call to talk about you." She made a face. "It wasn't to ask me on a date or anything."

"Aw, he's trying, though." I gave her a weak smile, but really didn't know what else to say. Why was Cody calling her? And did he know the depth of her feelings for him? I knew that TJ knew I loved him, but I didn't know if he knew just how deeply I loved and adored him. It was an embarrassing and scary thought thinking he knew just how much I wanted him.

"How do I look?" Sally spun around in her cute, short black-and-white dress, and I grinned at her as she changed the subject.

"You look absolutely gorgeous and you know it."

"I do look pretty hot." She giggled as she flicked her hair behind her shoulders and smiled at me, her bright red lips glistening on her glowing face. Her big brown eyes were radiating confidence and her eyelashes looked longer than I'd ever seen them with her new mascara. Sally looked absolutely gorgeous and I knew that she was hoping that Cody, when he arrived, would notice as well. I didn't know what to think about that. Cody was my brother and I loved him, but I didn't think he deserved someone like Sally, at least not how he had been treating her recently. She deserved an amazing man who would sweep her off of her feet and show her that she was his world, and I wasn't sure if Cody was confident enough to be the man to do that.

"You look amazing as well." Sally grinned at me and then whistled. "Absolutely beautiful. Being engaged is really doing it for you. Have you also lost some weight?" She looked at me again and tilted her head.

"I've lost about ten pounds." I nodded and sighed. "I haven't really been able to eat or sleep," I admitted. "I haven't really been working out or dieting. I just have all this nervous pent-up energy."

"Oh no." Sally frowned and looked at me. "That doesn't sound good."

"I guess I just feel so frustrated." I lowered my voice. "You know how much I love TJ. You know that I want to be with him forever. You know that, well, he's the one who has had my heart forever. And, well, I feel like every day I spend with him, I fall in love with him deeper and deeper, but I also keep making a longer crack in my heart. I don't know how I'm going to survive after this ends." I bit down on my lower lip, my eyes wide as I stared at her. The empty, sinking feeling entered my stomach again and I took a deep breath. I could not cry now. I was fed up of crying. And I didn't want to ruin my makeup. Smeared mascara and eyeliner didn't look good. At all.

"Oh, honey." Sally's eyes widened in response to what I'd said. "You need to just leave him. You need to forget this whole arrangement. He's not good for your heart. I know you love him, but if he's making you feel bad about yourself, he's not worth it. There will be other men, Mila. You are beautiful. You are generous. You're funny. Smart. Shit, you're the perfect girl. Any man would be happy to be with you. Trust me. You will fall for someone much better."

"But none of them will be TJ," I said, my voice bleak.

"They will be better than TJ."

"There is no one better than TJ." I gulped. "He's my everything."

"But you're not his everything," Sally said softly, her face sympathetic. "Don't you want a man who will make you his everything?"

"I just want TJ to love me."

"Oh, we're messes." Sally sighed and grabbed my hand. "How did we get to this place? Both of us in love with men who can't seem to love us. What are we doing to ourselves?"

"I don't know."

"I don't want to be single forever." Sally's lips pursed. "And I don't want to be waiting on Cody forever either. What if it never happens? What if he never falls for me? What if I end up at fifty, never married, no kids, no loves, no nothing because I just waited around on him?"

"That won't happen," I said, but then as I spoke the words I realized the same thing could happen to me. What if I just waited around on TJ to somehow fall in love with me and be okay with it? How long would I wait? What if it never happened? What if he fell in love with someone else while I was here waiting? It would crush me, and even thinking about it made me feel sick. Imagining him with someone else, falling in love, telling her he adored her, holding her close, kissing her—oh, God, that would kill me. I would be devastated.

"What are you thinking about, Mila?" Sally asked softly. "You look like you just found out someone died."

"What if TJ falls in love with someone else? Marries her? What if TJ's not the problem? What if it's me? What if he just can't fall in love with me because I'm not the one for him?

"Let's see how tonight goes and then we should have a serious conversation. Neither of us can just stay in these positions. It's not healthy for us."

"I know." I nodded. "I need to talk to TJ as well. Need to tell him some stuff. Need to just be free to accept whatever happens next. I don't want to be living in this emotional turmoil anymore."

"Yeah, it's not healthy," Sally agreed and we just stared at each other for a few moments, both of us wondering what it was going to take to get the other one to step off of the ledge.

"WELL, DON'T YOU TWO LOOK pretty?" TJ walked over to me and gave me a quick kiss on the cheek as he got home. Then he walked over to Sally and gave her a hug. "Looks like I got home just in time."

"Yeah, just in time to not cook anything." I shook my head at him. "Lucky you."

"Did you really want my help cooking?"

"No," I laughed and he grinned down at me, his eyes glowing.

"I'm just going to go and change quickly," he said with a laugh and walked towards the bedroom. "I'll be back."

"Okay," I said and looked at Sally, who was smiling.

"Don't miss me too much," he said with another laugh and I shook my head at him.

"I'll try not to." I giggled and grabbed Sally's hand. "Let's go and get a drink. We deserve one."

"I'm down for that," she agreed and we headed towards the kitchen. "So, TJ seems like he is in a good mood."

"Yeah, he does," I agreed happily. "It's been nice this last week."

"That's good." She nodded. "How's it been going with his business deal? Have you met many of the shareholders and partners? How's his dad been?"

"To be honest, I haven't really seen his dad or anyone else since that party." I shrugged. "And every time I bring it up to TJ, he changes the subject."

"That's weird."

"Yeah, it is." I nodded and held up a bottle of wine in one hand and a bottle of vodka in the other. "What's your poison?"

"I need liquid courage tonight." Sally grinned. "I'll have a vodka-Sprite."

"I think I'll have the same." I laughed and put the bottle of wine down. "So yeah, I'm not really sure how it's going."

"Four weeks is going to be up soon, though." Sally looked thoughtful. "I'm guessing that this arrangement is going to last longer, then?"

"We haven't really discussed it." I shrugged, but I knew that I was hopeful inside. I was hopeful that it would last forever. Well, not the engagement. I was hoping the engagement would last long enough to become real and then we'd get married.

"I guess nothing's happening yet?" she said uncertainly. "What about work? Are your parents doing better?"

"I don't think so." I sighed. "And I know they don't want to tell Nonno and worry him."

"Are you going to tell him?"

"I don't think so." I shook my head. "That's up to my parents."

"Yeah, I guess so. But aren't you majority owner?"

"I don't really like bringing that up." I bit down on my lower lip. "And it's not like it means much until I'm thirty anyways. That's when the shares vest."

"That just means that's when you can access the money. You still have all the rights as majority shareholder, Mila." Sally pursed her lips. "Maybe you should ask TJ if he can give you some advice and help."

"I don't want to do that." I shook my head. "It seems like it would be overstepping."

"That's not overstepping." She sighed. "Maybe he can help."

"Yeah, maybe."

"Any word on Barbie?" she asked casually and I shook my head.

"I have no care to ever hear her name again." I made a face and handed Sally her drink before downing mine. "No care at all."

"Yeah." She laughed and downed her drink as well.

Ding-dong.

"I guess Cody's here," I said as I put my drink down and walked towards the front door. "You going to be okay?"

"I'll be fine," Sally said as she took a deep breath. "God, I hope I don't make a fool of myself."

"You won't." I grinned at her. "I'll make sure you don't." I winked at her and then continued on my way and opened the door. "Hey, bro," I said and gave him a hug.

"Hey, you." He kissed me on the cheek and surveyed my face. "You look happy."

"I am happy." I nodded and then noticed that there were two guys standing next to him. "Hi, I'm Mila," I said as I stepped away from him.

"Oh, yeah, this is Brody and this is James," Cody said as he nodded to his two handsome friends. "I hope you don't mind that I invited them."

"It's no problem." I smiled at him, but inside I was shouting. I hoped I had made enough food.

"Great," he said and grinned at me. I saw his eyes searching inside the apartment and then he stopped when he saw Sally. "Hey, Sally, I was wondering if you were going to be here."

"She's my best friend, of course she was going to be here," I said, answering for her. "Are there going to be any other surprise guests tonight?" I gave Cody a look and he looked confused.

"Like who?"

"Barbie?" I hissed.

"Oh, she's got a boyfriend." He shrugged. "I guess she's dating some rich, older dude."

"What?" I frowned. "Already?"

"I don't know the story, but she had my watch and I wanted it back and, well, she said her 'rich, older boyfriend' wouldn't appreciate me coming over to get it."

"Okay." I shook my head but didn't continue the conversation. I didn't want Sally to hear us talking about Barbie and be reminded of his dalliance.

"Hi, guys." Sally did a sexy strut towards the four of us and I could see that all of the guys' attention was on her and her long legs in the heels she was wearing.

"Hi, I'm Brody." The tall, stocky blond guy stood forward and shook her hand.

"Hi, Brody." Sally gave him a dazzling smile. "Nice to meet you."

"You too, my dear, you too." He was grinning at her and continued to stand close to her.

"And this is James." Cody looked at Brody with an annoyed expression on his face.

"Nice to meet you, James." Sally smiled at him as well and he gave her a soft smile before turning to me.

"Hi, I'm James," he said, his big blue eyes sparkling as he gazed at me.

"Mila. Cody's sister, if you didn't figure that out yet."

"You're much prettier than him," he said, and I laughed.

"That's good to hear. Thank you." I blushed as he continued to smile at me.

"You're very welcome," he said as he ran his hand through his short, wavy brown hair. "Thanks for having us."

"You're very welcome," I said.

"He's very welcome for what?" TJ's voice came booming into the room.

"For Mila being so gracious as to have me over for dinner," James spoke up, his eyes never leaving mine.

"Sorry, who are you?" TJ frowned as he gazed at James and then at Brody.

"TJ, this is Brody and this is James. They are in my baseball league. We were batting earlier and I figured they could come for dinner as well. The more the merrier, right?" Cody said nonchalantly and I could see TJ's eyes narrowing at him. Hmm, I wonder what was going on there.

"Sure." TJ shrugged and walked over to me and kissed me on the lips. "I hope you didn't miss me too much."

"I didn't." I smiled up at him and his eyes narrowed.

"That's what you say now," he said softly, then turned back around. "Okay, who wants a drink?"

"I thought you would never ask, bro." Brody laughed and then looked at Sally. "What are you drinking tonight, beautiful?"

"I think I'm sticking with vodka-Sprites for now." Sally beamed at him and I could see Cody frowning at their exchange.

"And what about you?" James looked at me. "Actually, let me guess."

"Go on, then." I smiled as we all walked farther into the apartment. TJ was standing to my left and James was standing to my right.

"I think you look like a white-wine girl. Am I right?" He stared into my eyes with a teasing expression and I laughed.

"Actually tonight I'm drinking vodka as well." I smiled back at him and I felt TJ's hand on my arm.

"And she prefers red wine to white wine," TJ spoke up. "Nice guess, though. What do you want, James?" TJ had a smile on his face, but his voice was slightly gruff.

"I'll take a whiskey neat," James replied, a huge smile still on his face. "What is cooking, by the way? It smells amazing in here."

"I'm making my famous roast chicken with roast potatoes and baked macaroni and cheese with a salad."

"Oh, my God, that sounds amazing." James licked his lips. "Marry me."

"Ha ha ha," I laughed and blushed.

"Mila, let's get the drinks," TJ said and grabbed my hand, pulling me towards the kitchen.

"Okay," I said, annoyed at his attitude. "What do you want, Brody?"

"I'll have a whiskey as well."

"I'll take a beerski," Cody said and I saw Sally giving him a quick glance.

"Sounds good," I said and walked over to the fridge.

"Are you paying attention to the food?" TJ said as I took a beer out.

"Sorry, what?" I looked at him, confused.

"Maybe pay more attention to the food and less time flirting," TJ said as he grabbed his decanter of whiskey. "I don't think any of us want burnt food for dinner."

"I am paying attention to the food," I said, annoyed. "I don't even know what you're talking about."

"I'm just making sure," he said as he put two ice cubes in his glass and poured.

"Well, thanks for making sure," I said and left the kitchen and handed Cody his beer. "Here you go." I handed it to Cody, but he wasn't paying attention to me, as he was too busy watching Brody flirting with Sally, who was laughing her head off at something he was saying.

"Here are the whiskeys." TJ followed me out and handed a glass to James and Brody. They nodded their thanks and both started sipping their drinks.

"So are you guys hungry? I have bread and cheese for an appetizer." I looked at James and Brody.

"You had me at 'cheese'," James said and I smiled at him.

"Well you're easy to please, then." I laughed. "And to clarify, it's French bread and Brie."

"Even better." He grinned. "Tell me that you have strawberry or raspberry jam as well and I'll be an extremely happy man."

"I think we do." I laughed. "Though I'll have to check."

"I have strawberry jam," TJ said thinly. "Mila just moved in with me, so she doesn't know the complete contents of my fridge yet."

"You guys roommates?" James asked curiously.

"Something like that." I laughed and TJ scowled.

"What do you do, James?" TJ asked him, stepping closer to him. "Garbage man?" he said under his breath, and I gave him a quick glance.

"Sorry, what?" James asked with a cheery smile.

"What's your job?" TJ asked again and his eyes looked at me as he spoke.

"Oh, I'm an attorney. Patent litigation." James grinned. "You're in business, right? Cody was telling us."

"Yeah." TJ nodded and then smiled. "Mila's in retail therapy."

"Sorry, what?" James looked at me and half-smiled. "You work in retail?"

"Somewhat," I said and tried not to glare at TJ. "I work for my family company."

"She kinda works," TJ said. "She likes to shop a lot more. So any guy she dates should have a lot of credit cards."

"TJ." Sally spoke up for me and glared at him. "Stop being an asshole."

"I'm just joking," he said and laughed, though he still looked slightly pissed off.

"I don't mind spoiling my girlfriends," James said as he walked closer to me. "In fact, I consider it a pleasure."

"Oh yeah?" I smiled at him, trying to be beguiling, trying to annoy TJ for embarrassing me like that.

"So do I," Brody said to Sally with a huge grin as he sidled up closer to her. "In fact, I think I plan a pretty good first date as well."

"Oh yeah?" she said with a grin.

"Yeah." He stared into her eyes. "I'd like to take you on one sometime."

"Brody." Cody slapped his friend around the shoulder. "Sally doesn't want a player like you," he said with a smile on his face, but as I stared at my brother's tense face, I had the feeling that he was very jealous. *Hmm, interesting.*

"Mila, is the food nearly ready?" TJ asked me, his eyes narrowed. "I think we're all ready to eat."

"I'm not hungry for food," Brody said and licked his lips as he stared at Sally's legs, and I watched as Cody glared at him.

"Don't be a pig," James said and gave me a small smile. "Excuse my friend. He can't contain himself around a beautiful girl."

"And you can?" Brody said with a laugh.

"I'm doing so right now, aren't I?" James answered and then looked at me. "I think I'm being a gentleman—right, Mila?"

"Oh yes, I think—"

"Mila, let's go and check the food." TJ grabbed my hand and pulled me toward the kitchen. I followed behind him quickly, feeling slightly amused that he was jealous. "Is it ready?" he asked me, glaring at me as we walked into the kitchen.

"Unlikely," I said as I rolled my eyes at him and opened the oven. "There's no need to be rude to our guests, TJ."

"I'm not being rude," he said as he stood there and poured some more whiskey. "I'm sure they're hungry, just as I am."

"Yeah, you weren't complaining of hunger when you got home."

"I didn't want to be rude." He shrugged.

"TJ." I rolled my eyes at him. "You're jealous."

"Jealous of what?" He shook his head at me, his eyes looking slightly pissed still.

"Nothing," I said as I ladled some gravy over the chicken to baste it, before covering it again and pushing it back into the oven. "It's not ready, like I said."

"Well, just make sure you're paying attention to the guests as well as the food."

"Yes, sir, no sir, three bags full, sir."

"Keep calling me, sir, Mila." TJ's eyes sparkled at me.

"And what will happen if I do?" I put my hands on my hips and stared at him. "Huh?"

"You really wanna know?" His lips tilted up to the right.

"Yes, sir," I said and licked my lips naughtily at him.

"Come with me," he growled and grabbed my hand.

"Where are we going?" I opened my eyes innocently at him.

"I should take you to the living room, and give everyone a show." He pulled me towards him and leaned down and kissed me roughly. "But I'm not going to do that."

"I wouldn't let you do that." I kissed him back passionately and bit down on his lower lip.

"You wouldn't let me, huh?" he said before sucking on my tongue. I reached my hands up and ran my fingers through his hair and pulled on his silky tresses as I pushed my body against his chest and felt his warmness against me.

"Nope," I whispered against his lips, and he groaned.

"Come," he said and he pulled me out of the kitchen and down towards the bedroom.

"TJ," I whispered. "Where are we going?"

"You know where," he said as he opened the bedroom door and then pushed me inside before closing it.

"TJ, the food might burn, plus we have guests."

"So?" He grinned at me wickedly. "Who cares about a little burnt food?"

"James might," I said innocently and his eyes narrowed.

"Mila, Mila, Mila," he said softly and he pushed me down on the bed. "Legs up."

"Legs up?" I asked with a curious frown and kept my legs down.

"Legs up." He nodded and I watched as he unzipped his belt and pulled his hard cock out. It stuck out of his pants proudly and I swallowed hard as I stared at it. Boy, was it beautiful, and I was not a woman who thought penises were particularly attractive.

"Legs up or what?" I giggled, and he growled as he stepped forward and pulled my dress up. I felt his hands sliding up under my dress and he started to pull my panties down. "TJ," I said throatily. "We shouldn't do this."

"We shouldn't?" he asked with an evil grin and then he leaned down and I felt his tongue in between my legs and all I could do was start moaning as my legs spread to give him easier access. All thoughts of our guests and my dinner left my mind as his tongue licked up and down my wetness.

"Oh, my God," I cried out as I felt TJ's tongue entering me slowly and my body trembled as I clutched the bed sheets. "TJ," I cried out and he looked up at me and grinned.

"Shh, Mila. You don't want our guests to wonder what's happening."

"TJ." My eyes rolled in my head as I felt his mouth back against my wetness, and this time he was sucking on my throbbing bud. I closed my eyes again to concentrate on the feelings and I felt like my whole body was going to burst. I could feel my orgasm building up and I was just dying for a release. And then TJ stood up straight and just stared at me. "TJ," I moaned louder, making a face at him. "Please."

"Please what?"

"TJ," I groaned. "Please."

"You know what to do." He grinned down at me and licked his lips.

"TJ."

"That's my name," he said and then he started humming.

"TJ! What are you doing?"

"I'm about to start singing "Move Together" by James Bay."

"TJ," I moaned and watched as he grinned wider as I put my legs up in the air.

"Yes, Mila?" he said as he stepped forward and grabbed my legs and put them over his shoulder.

"Oh TJ," I said and closed my eyes and waited to feel him inside of me.

"Tell me what you want, Mila," he said, his voice throaty. My eyes fluttered open and looked up at him. He was staring down at me, his face looking more handsome than I'd ever seen him.

"Fuck me, TJ," I said and grinned.

"Louder." He winked at me.

"Fuck me, TJ," I said a little louder.

"Even louder."

"TJ, no." I shook my head.

"Louder," he said and I felt the tip of his cock rubbing against my clit. "What do you want, Mila? Tell me what you want."

"I already told you," I moaned as I tried to close my legs around him. "Please."

"Tell me again."

"TJ," I groaned and reached down and grabbed his cock and tried to guide it inside of me.

"Yes, Mila," he groaned as I squeezed his hardness and placed it against my entrance. "Shit, you're so wet."

"I want you, TJ. Please," I moaned and I was rewarded with the swift movement of him entering me.

"Is this what you wanted?" He groaned as he slammed in and out of me quickly, his hands around my ankles as he held my legs up. I could feel my whole body moving back and forth on the bed as he fucked me hard, each thrust seeming to enter me deeper and deeper.

"Yes," I cried out and I couldn't stop myself from screaming as I felt his finger reaching down to rub my clit quickly as he entered me. "TJ," I screamed out as I felt myself reaching the top of the cliff even faster than I'd thought possible. "Oooh," I screamed as he thrust into me even harder and deeper and I felt my whole body shaking as I started climaxing.

"Come for me, Mila," he groaned as I felt his body shuddering next to me. "Oh yes," he groaned and I felt him thrust into me three more times before pulling out and coming on my dress. "Oh Mila, shit," he groaned as he leaned down and kissed me on the lips.

"Oh, TJ," I giggled as I looked into his satiated eyes. "I'm going to have to change."

"I can wipe it off," he said as he kissed me again.

"I think I'll change." I moaned. "I hope no one asks why."

"Just say I got my sperm on you." He winked.

"You want Cody to kill you?"

"Okay, just say you got gravy on your dress. Ha ha." He stood up and pulled me up off of the bed. "Take your dress off and change."

"You're so bossy." I rolled my eyes at him as he zipped himself up.

"Isn't that what you love about me?" he asked with a smile and I just smiled back at him as I pulled my dress off. I wanted to answer him and tell him that that was just one of many things I loved about him, but I didn't want to ruin the mood and make it too serious by gushing on about how much I loved everything about him.

"Let me get changed and finish up dinner," I said and hit him on the shoulder instead. "Go and take care of our guests and I'll be out in a few minutes."

"Yes, ma'am," he said and saluted me. "Look who's being bossy now."

"NOW THAT'S WHAT I CALL a good dinner party." TJ closed the door behind Cody and Sally as they left and then turned to me. "Thank you for a delicious dinner."

"You're welcome." I smiled at him happily. "It was fun—well, aside from when you almost punched James."

"I didn't almost punch him. I just told him that maybe he should join an online dating service if he was looking that hard for a girlfriend." He shrugged and then stared at me. "Or were you hoping to be that girlfriend?"

"Whatever, TJ." I rolled my eyes at him. "You're an idiot for even saying that."

"I'm an idiot for you." He smiled at me with an adorable puppy face and I just shook my head.

"I have dishes to do." I sighed and ignored his cutesy words. He was drunk and I didn't want to take anything he said right now too seriously. He'd been loving and attentive all evening and my body still felt high from our lovemaking, but I didn't want to read anything into it. I already knew that he was weird with his feelings and as far as I knew it was the alcohol putting him out of character.

"Leave the dishes until the morning and we'll do them together," he said and put his arm around my waist. "Let's go to bed and have some lovemaking."

"TJ." I leaned my head against his shoulder. "You look like you're way too drunk for any lovemaking to me."

"I'm never too drunk for lurvemaking," he said and he slurred his words.

"Uh huh," I said as we walked towards the bedroom. "We'll see." We walked in companionable silence in the room and I watched as he pulled off all of his clothes and jumped into bed. He lay flat on his back, looked up at me and grinned as he closed his eyes and stretched.

"You're so tired," I said, smiling down at him, a feeling of affection sweeping through me as I gazed at him.

"I wouldn't say so tired," he mumbled, his eyes still closed.

"Oh, wouldn't you?" I said softly, smiling to myself as I took my dress off and put on a nightgown. I walked out of the bedroom and went to the bathroom so I could take my makeup off. That was something Sally had instilled in me. Always try and remove makeup at night; especially eye makeup, because it did terrors to your skin if you left it on when you went to sleep. I cleaned my face and then walked back to the bedroom feeling happy, but still slightly anxious. Everything was going so well, but it was all really a facade. Nothing had really changed between us. I sighed to myself as I wondered if I was doing the right thing staying here and playing this game. Was I only prolonging the pain I was going to feel in just a few weeks? I crawled into bed and snuggled next to TJ. He rolled over, pulled me towards him and held me against his chest and moaned slightly. I snuggled next to him and listened to the sound of his heartbeat as I lay there.

"If I ever wanted to get married, it would be to someone like you," he mumbled next to my ear and I froze and looked up at him. His eyes, though still sleepy, were open now.

"Why don't you want to get married?" I looked at TJ, truly curious as to why he was so opposed to a union I couldn't wait to enter.

"Because a marriage is meant to last forever," he said without pause, his eyes finding mine as he tried to focus on me.

"And that freaks you out? Being with the same person forever?"

"No." He shook his head and frowned, sleepiness making me confused. "What freaks me out is the possibility that the marriage could end. What freaks me out is that I could have the one person I love more than anything in the world and I could lose her. Marriages aren't infallible. People change, fall out of love. It happens every day. My heart would break, my world would end. I would cease to be the person I am if that were to happen." He shook his head. "I will not let myself become a statistic."

"Your marriage might not end," I said, but I felt weird saying the words. I wanted to say *our* marriage would not end, but I knew that would be putting all my cards on the table and I wasn't willing to do that.

"But the love might," he said with a yawn and I watched as his eyes fluttered closed again and he drifted back to sleep.

Chapter Eleven

TJ

Two Years Ago

"WHEN I MEET THE MAN of my dreams, I want him to woo me with flowers and chocolates and poems." Mila laughed as she spoke to Sally in the living room.

"Poems?" I spoke up and sat on the couch next to them. "What sort of pansy is going to be writing you poems?"

"A man full of romance." Mila rolled her eyes at me. "A man who loves me more than life itself."

"You've been reading too many of those romance books, Mila." I shook my head. "I don't know any guy who's writing love poetry."

"I know plenty of guys that do," Sally said with an encouraging smile. "Don't listen to TJ. He's just jaded because he doesn't have a romantic bone in his body."

"I know. He doesn't." Mila stuck her tongue out at me and laughed. "When I fall in love and meet my soul mate, I want to be so special to him that he'd give up his life for me."

"Give up his life, huh?"

"Yup." She grinned. "He would give up his life, his happiness, his everything just to be with me."

"Would he give up his dog?" I asked with a grin.

"If he had to," she said, not even blinking.

"Would he give up his car?"

"That's not even a question."

"Would he give up his job?" I continued, grinning.

"He'd give up everything because he loves me so much."

"Would you really want a guy who would give up everything just to be with you? He sounds like a bit of a loser. Have some self-respect, man."

"He does have self-respect." Mila frowned at me. "He'll just love me so much that nothing else matters but making me happy."

"Good luck with that," I said and reached for the remote control. "You might be waiting a long time."

"I know you don't believe in soul mates, but I do," she said wistfully, her expression changing. "I just want to meet that one guy who will think of me first. I want to meet that one guy who truly cares about my feelings, my wants, my life. I want that guy who wakes up and smiles thinking about me and falls asleep listening to my voice. I want that one guy who loves me so much that all he cares about is putting a smile on my face and will do anything to make me laugh because seeing me happy would make him happy."

"Yeah," Sally agreed. "I'd love to meet a guy like that as well."

"You girls are living in fantasy land." I laughed at them. "Those guys do not exist."

"Just because you're not like that doesn't mean they don't exist," Mila said and hit me in the arm. "Stop trying to burst our bubbles."

"I'm not trying to burst your bubbles, but guys aren't like that. We do what we want to get what we want. First thing on our minds is sex, then maybe food, then work, then sex again." I laughed at their open mouths. "I'm just being honest. I've never done anything for love. Most guys are not going to put themselves out of their comfort zone for no reward. It just doesn't work like that."

"When a guy is in true love, he will do anything and everything for the woman he loves," Mila said softly. "Just to make her happy. If even for one day. Even if it meant he would lose her. A man in true love cares only about doing everything he can to protect and cherish his woman. And that will be the only thing in his mind." She just stared at me then and I stared back at her silently. Who was I to argue with her? I sat back and I could feel my heart pounding and I could feel myself starting to feel sad. What would it feel like to be a man in love like that? What would it feel like to be the man in love with Mila like that? I wasn't sure that I'd ever want to find out. It seemed like it would be way more than I'd want to deal with.

Present Day

"HOW MUCH DO I LOVE you?" I looked at Mila's profile photo on Facebook for what seemed like the tenth time in the last couple of hours. I stared into her wide-eyed gaze and smiled at the cute cheeky smile in the photo as she stuck her tongue out. "Oh, my Mila." I sighed and closed the tab and shut my laptop down. I couldn't spend the day staring at her photos again. I didn't even use Facebook or other social media much. I didn't care about it. I liked to live my life in private, but that hadn't stopped me from spending hours on the site in the last few days, trying to figure out what she was doing, where she was going, how she was feeling. She hadn't made it easy for me, though. She hadn't updated her page in over a month, so to placate myself I'd spent my hours looking at her old posts and old photos. I wasn't sure why I'd become this obsessed person. I knew I could get the answers I wanted just by talking to her, but then what would that accomplish? I knew I couldn't give her any of the answers that she wanted.

I looked down at the files on my desk and grimaced. D-day was nearly here. I had to sign the paperwork within 24 hours and that would mean that my father would officially own Mila's parents' company and legally there would be nothing that anyone could do about it.

Knock knock.

"Come in," I said as I looked up at the door, hoping it wasn't my father about to walk in and pressure me into signing the papers right now. I'd throw them in his face if it was him.

"Why, hey, stud." Barbie sauntered into the room and my stomach dropped.

"Hi." I nodded, not smiling. "How can I help you, Barbie?"

"Is that any way for you to treat your ex-lover?" She sashayed over to my desk and leaned forward, her breasts sticking out towards me.

"We were never lovers." I glared at her. "What do you want?"

"To change that." She grinned and she moved around to the side of my desk. "We can become lovers now."

"Barbie, what do you want?" I said, annoyed, as I felt her hand on my shoulder.

"I just told you." She leaned over and whispered in my ear, "I want you to fuck me deep and hard."

"I'm going to give you ten seconds to get out of my office," I said and pursed my lips. What the hell did my father see in this woman? She was nothing but an opportunistic slut.

"Really, TJ? Is that how you're going to speak to me?" She stood up straight and laughed, then I felt her hand on my thigh, running up my leg. "I guess now you're getting some from your little friend, Mila. Well, I guess I shouldn't say little, she's not exactly a size zero is she?" She laughed loudly and my body grew still. "But I guess now that your plus-size friend is giving it up to you, you're too good for me."

"Barbie, I'm only going to ask you this one more time, what do you want?"

"You know what I wonder," she said and sat on the side of my desk. "I wonder why you're leading this girl on. I mean, I get it, men want sex, but really, anyone can see that idiot is in love with you. And she has no idea who you are or what you're doing, does she?" She laughed as she gazed at me. "You think you're better than me and your father, but are you really? Leading her on, fucking her, making it hard for her to ever forget you. Is that what a good guy does, TJ?"

"What's it to you?" I stared at her, my heart pounding as I realized some of what she was saying was true. How was I any better than her or my dad? Mila had no idea what was going on, really, and that was because of me. And yes, I knew she loved me and yes, I wanted her to love me, but I didn't have anything else to offer in return. Nothing, but heartache and heartbreak and I wasn't going to pretend that I had anything more.

"Your dad and I want this deal to happen." Her eyes narrowed and it was then that I knew my dad had sent her in to take care of the situation. He was probably worried that I was going to back out of the deal. Little did he know, I was a hundred percent in at this point.

"I know that," I said and stood up. "That's why you're here?"

"We worked hard to make this happen." She slid off the desk and stared at me. "I put up with that bimbo for a whole weekend and slept with her brother just to make sure that he was occupied. Don't make it be for nothing."

"You slept with Cody because you're easy." I didn't hold back my distaste for her.

"That and because I loved to see the look on that bitch Sally's face the morning after." She threw her head back and laughed. "Oh, the jealousy in her eyes. I would have loved to have seen that look in Mila's eyes as well. Could you imagine if she caught us fucking in the shower? She'd still be bawling her eyes out."

"Get out." I pointed towards the door.

"Aww, seems like you've actually got some feelings left in you still." She stared at me, her eyes cold. "It's a pity that you became weak and let yourself fall for her. It will make it harder on you when she walks away for good."

"Excuse me?"

"You know she'll never talk to you again, right?" She laughed gleefully. "You can't seriously think you guys will go back to how it was before? Don't be an idiot, TJ."

"This is none of your business."

"Oh, it is very much my business." The smile left her face and she looked at me coldly. "And I'm going to make sure everything goes according to plan. No matter what I have to do or say . . ." Her voice trailed off. "Capiche?"

"Leave my office." I turned away from her, my whole body cold. It had suddenly hit me that Barbie was correct about something I'd never considered. What if Mila never spoke to me again? That wasn't something I'd been prepared for. I knew that I'd lose our physical relationship and possibly her love, but losing her from my life forever? That was unthinkable. Unimaginable. How could I live without her in my life forever? What sort of life would that be? I heard Barbie finally leaving my office, but I didn't even look back. I had greater concerns on my mind now. I picked up the phone and made a call, my heart in my throat.

"TJ?" Nonno's voice was subdued.

"We need to talk."

"I've been waiting for this call." He sighed.

"Can I come over?"

"Okay," he said stiffly. "I'll be here."

"I'll be there in about thirty minutes," I said and then hung up, picking up the file from my desk, my briefcase and jacket and leaving the office. I needed to speak to Nonno and I needed to see if I could somehow make this right.

"TJ, WOULD YOU LIKE ANYTHING to drink?" Nonno asked me softly as I sat down on the couch.

"Some water, thanks." I nodded and watched as he walked slowly to the kitchen. I looked around his familiar living room and stared at the photos of Mila as a kid, smiling at her happy face.

"Here we go," he said as he handed me a glass and sat down next to me. "So how can I help you?"

"I don't know that Mila is very happy right now," I said stiffly, not sure what to say.

"She's going through an emotional turmoil." Nonno nodded and leaned back. "She loves you a lot, so this is hard for her."

"It's hard for me too." I sipped my water. "I don't know that I can go through with this."

"TJ, Mila is my granddaughter, and I love her deeply. I would do anything for her. I do not like to see her hurt. I do not like to see her in pain." He stopped and just stared at me.

"This was your idea, Nonno." I sighed. "I didn't want to go through with this."

"You must." Nonno said simply. "Her parents are running the business into the ground. There will be nothing left when they are done. The money from your father's investment will keep Mila afloat for the rest of her life."

"But she doesn't even know. Isn't there another way?"

"She would never go behind her parent's back and I, I can't." He sighed and leaned back. "You must continue with the deal."

"I just hate that I'm giving my father what he wants and doing it so deceitfully." I closed my eyes. "She's going to hate me. She's going to think I did this for me and my dad."

"She loves you." Nonno's voice was soft. "This wasn't all about the money, you know. This arrangement . . ." He sighed and I opened my eyes and looked at him.

"I have nothing else to offer her, Nonno. I told you that. I told you that before you told me to get into this arrangement. I don't like having these secrets from her. I don't want her to think everything has been a huge lie."

"TJ, you are like a grandson for me. I know you've had a hard life, but try and let her in. All love is not bad. All pain is not bad. Mila is strong. She can handle a relationship. She can handle good times and bad."

"I don't want her to have bad times." I bit down on my lower lip. "She's going to hate me when she finds out everything I've been hiding from her."

"She'll know soon enough." Nonno rubbed his forehead.

"And then her heart will break forever and she'll never speak to me again." I said, my heart sinking as I realized everything that I was going to be giving up.

"We're doing this for Mila." Nonno said. "We're doing this because I can't see her unhappy. I can't see her worrying and wondering. I just can't. I've always been her rock."

"I know." I nodded. "I know."

"You must do this for me, TJ. You must." He grabbed my hand. "This is for Mila. If she were to know everything. If her parents were to know. It would all go wrong. You know this. You know this is the only way."

"I know." I said again.

"Take her to the lake or the beach tonight." He continued. "Make it a special night. You know she loves nature."

"I know."

"Do this for her, TJ. If you love her, in some way, which I know you do. Make it special. Make it special before it hurts. Because we both know it's going to hurt. If you love her in your heart, if you want the best for her, even if you don't want to tell her. Do this. Do this for her. This is what we must do. This is what we do because she's the most special person in our lives."

I just stared at him then. I didn't know what to say. I didn't know how to tell him that I didn't know if this was about Mila or more about him. However I kept my mouth shut. What did I know about feelings and love? Who was I to tell him that the things he was doing out of love were the things that would most probably break her heart more than anything else?

Chapter Twelve

Mila

WORDS CONSUMED MY MIND. THOUGHTS, dreams, questions— everything I wanted to know was trapped in my brain, wanting to come out, wanting to be said, but silence enveloped us. I kept my eyes on the sky, dark blue with blinking yellow stars taunting me in their glory. I felt him shifting next to me, his shoulder brushing mine as he moved. For the briefest second, I felt the momentary shock of electricity that always struck me when we touched. My shoulder tingled but my hands stood still, fighting the urge to reach out and touch his hand. The wind was cool now, blowing against my skin as if taunting me too.

I closed my eyes for the briefest of seconds as my stomach churned. "I love you" spun through my mind as I lay there. *I love you. How badly I wanted to say the words. Do you love me? Do you think you could love me? If I had to wait a million years for you to love me, I'd wait.* Of course, I didn't say anything. That was too pathetic. I was too pathetic. I couldn't fix him. Especially not when he didn't even seem to want to acknowledge what we had. He didn't want to let me in. Not in the way that I wanted him to. I opened my eyes slowly and stared back up at the sky. The trees seemed ominous as I stared up. I could see the shadow of an owl in one of the branches above me. I stared up at it, wanting to fixate on the owl, instead of the man next to me.

"I always feel like I'm the only man in the world when I come to the woods," TJ said finally, his voice sounding distant, even though he was a mere inch from me.

"The only man in the world?" I asked softly, wanting to turn to look at him, but remaining on my back, in a neutral position.

"Maybe it's a dream," he said. "To be one with nature, to just live with the land, let the worries of the everyday world consume someone else for once."

"I'd like to climb that tree." I pointed up. "And I'd like to sit on the highest branch and just stare out at all the trees and let the beauty and tranquility take me away." I bit down on my lower lip to stop myself from saying something I shouldn't. I wanted to ask him what his worries were. I wanted him to share them with me. I wanted to fill that void in his life. But I didn't know how to. I felt like I had put myself out there so much already and yet, I wasn't really any closer to him. Yes, I felt we were more intimate and sometimes I felt like I was actually a real part of his life, but there was so much he still had hidden. He hadn't even told me why we'd come out to the forest for the evening.

"Take you away where?" He rolled over and I could feel him staring at me.

"Anywhere?" I said, a throb of emotion escaping through my voice.

"I don't want you to go anywhere," he said softly and I could feel his face moving closer to me. "Look at me, Mila." I felt his hands on my shoulder and I rolled over to look at him. His green eyes were dark in the light, but I could still see the light sparkle as he gazed at me searchingly. "What are you thinking?" he asked me after a few seconds, his face an expression of melancholy and curiosity.

"If I could survive in the woods by myself," I said quickly, staring back into his eyes intently. I looked to the side as my real thoughts tumbled through my brain. *What do I mean to you, TJ? What do I really mean to you?*

"You could survive," he said and I felt his fingers on my face. "Look at me." He turned me to face him. "You could survive anything."

I couldn't survive you not loving me.

"We should go camping next week," he said and smiled briefly. "We'll go to Yosemite."

"Maybe." I nodded and smiled back briefly.

"I wonder sometimes if anyone sees me, who I really am." He lay back and I could hear the emotion in his voice. "There are things, Mila, things you don't understand. Things that make this complicated."

"It doesn't have to be complicated." My breath caught.

"I'm not the man for you, Mila. I'm not looking for the same things."

"You don't even know what I'm looking for."

"A true love. A real love. A soul mate. Someone who will captivate your heart. Someone who will say all the right things. Someone who will be there for you when you need them. Someone who can listen. Someone that can provide for you. Love you. Truly. Deeply. With his whole heart. Someone who makes you his world. Someone who's in a place to hold you close and never let go. That's what you're looking for. That's what you deserve. That's the type of man you need. You need someone who doesn't have thoughts constantly running through his head. You need someone who doesn't have something to prove. You know, someone who knows how to love like that."

All I want is you. I don't care how little of you I have. The words caught in my throat. How could I make him see that every part of him was what I wanted?

"Say something, Mila." He turned back to me, his face twisted. "Speak to me."

"I'd like to fly," I said. "If you could see me in the darkness, flying through the sky, you'd be amazed by me. You'd be amazed by all I could see and do."

"I see you in the light," he whispered. "And I see you in the darkness. That's the problem." His voice cracked and I closed my eyes, feeling like someone had just shot an arrow through my heart. Confusion and sorrow filled me. My heart of glass was cracking and I wasn't sure it would ever be whole again. "I can't bear to see you in the dark, Mila. I don't think I'd survive."

I can't survive without you ran through my head, but once again I didn't speak.

"The man who loves you shouldn't be the man who breaks your heart, Mila," he continued, as if he were trying to convince me of the reasons why I should be happy he didn't love me.

"Yeah," I said finally, trying not to cry. "I need to tell you something," I said finally. There was no time like the present and I needed to get everything off of my mind.

"Sure," he said and he rolled to look at me. "What is it?"

"I did something a long time ago and you might hate me for it."

"Oh?" His tone had changed and I looked over at him.

"There was a girl, when you were in college, one weekend when Sally and I were staying with you and Cody, and she came over and—"

"She told you she was pregnant with my baby." TJ grinned at me. "And you told her to leave like some badass bitch."

"You knew?" My jaw dropped open as my eyes widened. "You knew all this time and you never told me?"

"I'd never even slept with that girl." He laughed. "Yeah, I knew. I thought it was funny." He shrugged. "Has this been bothering you for a while?"

"I've been feeling guilty for years." I bit down on my lower lip. "It was a horrible thing to do."

"Oh, Mila." He reached over and held me and kissed my nose

softly. "I'm sorry, I should have mentioned something to you."

"I felt so bad for what I did, and for lying." I sighed. "I hate lying."

"I know." His eyes shifted away from mine and he sighed. "I hate lying too."

"Is there something you're not telling me, TJ?" I asked bravely, finally voicing the words I'd been wanting to say for a long time. "I feel like there's something going on. And I wish you'd share it with me."

"Mila, there are so many things I want to tell you." He looked back into my eyes. "You have to understand that."

"Things like what?"

"Things like how beautiful I think you are. How smart. How wonderful. How brilliant. How your smile lights up a room and my heart." He stopped as his phone started ringing and he sighed as he took it from his pocket. I saw a bunch of text messages on his phone and I watched him responding to them quickly. My heart raced as he turned the phone away from me so that I couldn't see the screen. Who was he texting? Did he have someone else? A girlfriend? Someone he really did like, or maybe even loved? My heart grew cold at the thought and I could feel myself starting to feel sick. Was that what TJ was hiding? The fact that he was seeing someone else? I lay back on the grass on my back and just stared up at the stars, trying to breathe in and out to calm my nerves.

"Sorry about that," TJ said, turning back to me.

"That's fine," I said quietly. "Who was it?"

"Oh," he paused. "Just some girl."

"Oh," I said, my stomach lurching, waiting for him to say more. "And you needed to text her back right away?" I said after he didn't say anything else.

"Yeah, I knew she'd keep calling and texting if I didn't." He sighed but still didn't say more.

"I see," I said, but I didn't. I felt like I wanted to die. Another woman added a whole new element to my heartache.

"She doesn't know I went out of town," he continued. "She wanted to talk to me."

"About what?" I asked softly and looked over into his eyes.

"You," he said softly, his face serious. "She wanted to talk about you."

"Oh," I said and I felt tears drifting down my face.

"It's complicated, Mila. It's just so complicated. I don't even know what to say anymore." He reached over and ran his fingers down my face and brushed away my tears. "Please don't cry."

"I'm not crying." I looked away from him.

"My mom used to say that when I caught her crying," he said abruptly, his eyes going dark. "I just remembered that. I would catch her sometimes, just crying, and I never knew why. She'd usually stop right away. And then she'd smile and hold me close and kiss me and tell me I was her perfect little boy." He smiled at me wryly. "Then if my dad caught her, he'd tell her to stop coddling me and she'd let me go and I'd just sit there, slightly confused and bereft, not understanding." He blinked up at me. "Then she just stopped hugging altogether, not unless she was sure my dad wouldn't see."

"Oh, TJ." My heart broke for him. "I'm so sorry."

"It's okay." He nodded. "That wasn't the part that hurt." He paused. "The part that hurt was seeing her hug and smile at everyone else. It made me feel small, unloved, like I'd done something wrong. I remember once, I had a party and she hugged all my school friends and asked each and every one of them how their day had been, yet she didn't even look me in the eyes. She didn't even care about me, her own son, the one she should have loved the most."

"I don't know why she did that," I whispered and stroked the side of his face. "I'm so sorry." The words sounded inadequate, even to my own ears.

"I was too young to understand that it must have been due to my dad," he said and sighed. "All I could think about was how she always used to hold me close and hug and kiss me until I couldn't breathe. And she'd tell me how much she loved me. How she couldn't imagine loving anyone more than me. And then she just stopped."

"I'm sure she didn't stop."

"She just stopped. I was her world. She told me I was her world. She used to tell me that I was her reason for living. That my birth was what had made her life perfect. She told me that the day she had me was the day she started to believe in God again. He'd proven he existed by giving her something so perfect." His throat caught. "And then she stopped loving me and she died."

"Oh, TJ." I pulled him into my arms and held him tightly. "You were the best thing that ever happened to her, but your dad and whatever other demons she had, well, that stopped her from being the person she was inside."

"Sometimes I wish I could talk to her," he said. "I'd like to know what happened. I'd like to know if she stopped loving me."

"She'd never stop loving you, TJ." I kissed him hard. "No one could stop loving you," I whispered against his lips. *I could never stop loving you*, I thought to myself as I dismissed the other girl from my thoughts. My heart was aching for my TJ, the man who still held the hurt and fears from his childhood.

"I want to make love to you," he muttered against my lips. "I need to be inside of you."

I didn't answer; instead, I slowly took off his shirt and then pulled his pants and boxers down. I then stood up and slowly undressed and threw my clothes to the ground. I looked down at his moon-kissed face and my heart swelled with love at the look of desire that shone back at me.

"Come to me, baby." He reached his arms up and I took his hands and straddled him. I felt his hardness between my legs and I rocked back and forth and teased myself with his manhood. He leaned up and pulled me down slightly so that he could cover my right nipple with his mouth and suck, while his hand played with my other breast. I stretched my body down against him and kissed his neck, while my hands played with his chest and ran down his slightly hairy stomach. My fingers played with his bellybutton and I gasped as he started nibbling on my nipple. I adjusted my body and sat up slightly and reached down and guided him into me hesitantly. This was the first time I was really the guiding force during intercourse and I was loving the feeling of power. As he slid inside of me, I found myself closing my eyes and moving back and forth on him gently, enjoying every stroke of him inside of me, as the stars shone down on us. The moment felt primal and raw and like we were one with nature.

"I'm flying, TJ," I cried out as I felt my orgasm building. My hair flew behind me and the wind cooled down my heated body.

"I'm flying as well, Mila." He grabbed a hold of my hips and moved my body back and forward even faster. I gyrated on him as hard as I could and I could feel both of our bodies trembling as we neared our crashing point. We cried out together as we both came and my body fell down on top of him as I climaxed.

"I love you, TJ," I said softly into his ear. "That will never change."

"I know," he whispered back. "That's my dream and my hope."

Chapter Thirteen

Mila

I WALKED ALONG THE SIDE of the river by myself, watching the sunrise. The previous evening had been touching and profound, but the sadness in my heart told me that things were never going to change. TJ was broken, even if he didn't know it. And he might never be able to love me in the way that I'd wanted. I knew it in the way he'd pulled away from me when we'd moved apart this morning. He'd looked embarrassed and sad, and even more than that, he'd looked vacant. That was what had broken me. I'd felt that after last night we were growing closer, but this morning it had seemed like we were further apart than ever before.

I walked over to the grass and sat down and then lay back and closed my eyes. I knew I couldn't stay here long. TJ had to get back to work. His phone had been ringing since about five a.m. and I'd heard him muttering that he'd be in the office as soon as possible. I wanted to ask him what was going on at work, but didn't want to seem like I was being nosey. Plus, that wasn't the conversation that I really wanted to have. I wanted to talk about us, about him. About what we were really doing. I wanted to tell him I wanted out. I didn't want to be his four-week fiancée anymore. Sally had been right. It was only four weeks, but I knew it was going to hurt for a lot longer than that. I was fighting a losing battle. TJ was never going to be mine and the pain that I felt every time I was with him was almost as much as the love. It was becoming too much for me to handle. I didn't want to feel this way anymore. I didn't want to feel like my whole day was made with his smile and my whole day was ruined with his frown.

I looked up as I heard footsteps approaching me. It was TJ. He was wearing a T-shirt and jeans and a lopsided smile on his face that looked nervous and anxious at the same time. It was weird to see him this way. I was so used to the man who always used to tease me and try and make fun of me. Seeing this vulnerable side of TJ made me see him as someone different, still wonderful and fun, but someone deeper and of more character. It was hard not to fall deeper in love with him, the more I saw of him, flaws and all. He walked towards me and sat next to me, not saying anything. I looked away from him and just stared at the sky and we just lay there in silence.

"I'll tell you a story," TJ said finally as he lay next to me in the grass.

"I don't want to hear a story." I didn't look at him as I shifted away from him. Why had he followed me here? Why couldn't he just leave me alone? Or just tell me that he needed to get back to the office and that we had to leave.

"There once was a girl. She loved a boy. With all her heart. All her soul. She loved him, even when she didn't know him. She loved him for everything he was. She loved him for everything he wasn't. She loved him for the way he smiled when she giggled. The way he frowned when he disapproved of something she was doing. The way he pursed his lips when he was cross. The way he held her hand when she was tipsy. She loved him for the way he always knew exactly how she felt. She loved him even when he didn't love her. She loved him with so much hope and wonder. And she waited. Patiently. She waited for the day when he would love her. In fairy tales, soul mates always came together. And she knew he was her soul mate. She knew as sure as there were stars in the sky that he was hers." TJ's voice broke and my lips trembled at his words. My eyes started to fill with tears. I hated him. I hated him for coming here and talking and saying things that made my heart hurt even more.

"So then what happened?" I asked him, my voice barely a whisper.

"He wasn't good enough."

"You mean he didn't love her," I interjected, fed up with his bullshit.

"I mean, he wasn't good enough." TJ sighed. "Life isn't always a fairy tale."

"No shit."

"There once was a boy," he said softly. "He loved a girl. With his whole being. With his whole heart and soul. He loved a girl to the point of distraction. He loved her to the point that he couldn't sleep. He loved her to the point that she was all he could think about. He loved her to the point where her smile kept him awake at night because it was so bright. He loved her to the point that it broke his heart that he made her sad. He loved her to the point of infinity, yet he couldn't tell her."

"Okay, and?" I turned to him then. I couldn't avoid looking at him anymore. I stared at his face, then his hair. I so badly wanted to reach over, touch his hair, touch his face, touch his lips.

"He didn't believe in magic. He didn't believe in the stars. He was afraid to fly." He rolled over and faced me. "He didn't believe . . ." His voice trailed off. "It's a long way to fall when you live in the clouds."

"Maybe you wouldn't fall." I blinked rapidly.

"There once was a boy." He stared directly into my eyes, a bleak expression burning into my soul. "He had a secret. He had a secret that he knew would break her heart. And he knew that the fall was inevitable."

"Maybe he should have trusted the girl." I closed my eyes and tried to ignore the racing of my heart. "Maybe he should have believed in the magic. Maybe he should have jumped out into the universe and screamed and shouted that he didn't care what happened. Maybe the boy shouldn't have been afraid to fly." I opened my eyes then. "We could have been in the air, barely breathing together. Risking it all." I gave him a small smile and jumped up. "Maybe he should have lived in the clouds with her."

"Mila." His voice broke as he jumped up as well. "You don't know what you're saying."

"I'm not afraid to fly, TJ. You are." I paused for a few seconds, wondering if this was finally going to be the end for both of us. "I love you," I said after a few more seconds, my voice cracking as I decided to put it all out there.

"I want you," he said.

"I need you," I said.

"I miss you every time I'm not with you," he said.

"I can't live without you," I said.

"I can't breathe without you," he said.

"I'm falling," I said.

"I'll catch you," he said.

"I'm tired," I said.

"I'll hold you," he said.

"I'm crying," I said.

"I'll wipe away your tears," he said.

"Love me," I said.

"Idontknowhattosay," he said.

"Just love me," I said.

"It'snotthateasy," he said.

"It is," I said.

"It isn't," he said.

"My heart is made of glass and you have just cracked it," I said melodramatically and hit him in the arm, hard. "I hate you for making me feel this way. I hate you." He just stared at me for about ten seconds and then his expression changed and he started laughing. "Oh, Mila, I'm a fool," he said as he stopped laughing.

"Why are you a fool?"

"I never wanted to fall in love with you. I never wanted to feel this way." He sighed. "I don't even know why I'm admitting this now."

"What are you admitting?" I asked hopefully, my breath in my throat, waiting patiently.

"I love you, Mila Brookstone. I don't know how or why, or what's going to happen, but I know as sure as there are tears in your eyes that I love you and I don't want to hurt you anymore. I couldn't bear to hurt you."

"You really love me?" I said slowly, not believing what I was hearing.

"I think it's been obvious." He sighed again. "I've just been scared to say the words. I've been scared to say it out loud because then that makes it real. And once it's real, it means it's in the universe. It's out there. I belong to you and you belong to me and we're in love. We're soul mates and that scares the shit out of me."

"It doesn't have to," I whispered and he just reached over and held my hands.

"After yesterday, talking to you about my mom, it made me realize so many things. It made me realize that a lot of my hurt and fear comes from my mom and dad's relationship. He was mentally abusive to her, emotionally abusive and she didn't know how to cope. I think she probably suffered from depression as well." He sighed. "And my dad did nothing to help. I hate him for the man that he is, but I also realized this morning when you left me in the bed and came out here, I didn't want to be him. And I didn't want to be the man hiding away from my feelings because I was scared. I love you, Mila. I love you like I've never loved anyone before in my life. We were destined to be together. I feel that in my soul. My very soul. Do you know that? Do you know how much you mean to me? How much you've always meant to me? It's scary," he said, his eyes blazing into mine.

"If I mean half as much to you as you mean to me, then yes, I know," I said, smiling at him.

"Look, there's something I need to tell you." His face changed to one of anguish and my heart froze.

"What is it, TJ?"

"I don't know how to tell you this." He sighed and I could see that he was worried. "It might change everything and I understand if it does, but I can't not tell you."

"You're scaring me, TJ. Please just tell me."

"So, all the calls I've been getting, and this whole engagement, well, it's not what you think."

"What are you talking about?" I asked, confused.

"Our engagement—it wasn't about me, or impressing the board, or any of that." He took a deep breath. "It's about your family's company. It's in trouble. Real trouble. Your parents will probably be bankrupt in the next three to six months. Nonno knew, has known for a while, that it's not doing well. They haven't listened to any of his advice, so he came to me." He took a deep breath. "He wanted me to help him make sure that his company, his investment and legacy to you didn't go down the drain."

"What are you talking about, TJ? How could it go down the drain? How could you help?"

"You have fifty-one percent of the shares in the company. You can make all the decisions."

"But that's just in name." I shook my head, still confused. "I haven't done anything."

"When we got engaged, you gave me power of attorney. I'm able to control the company." He gazed into my eyes. "Today I'm going to sign a contract that allows my father to purchase your company for ten million dollars. This is what Nonno wanted. This is what he wanted me to do. And he didn't want anyone to know. He knew your parents wouldn't do it. He knows that my dad might tear apart the company, but he doesn't care. He wants to make sure you're taken care of, Mila. He loves you with all his heart and, well, he can't live knowing that you might be left with nothing."

"What? What are you talking about? You're signing my family's company away to your dad?" My jaw dropped. "You used me?"

"I didn't want to do it. I haven't even done it yet. It's been killing me, Mila. I've been going back and forth on what to do. I feel like I'm betraying you every time I even think about the contract. I hate myself. I'm only doing it because I made a promise to Nonno. He begged me to help him with this. He said if I cared about you at all, I would do it because it was for your best interests." He sighed. "I agreed before I fully understood what it would be like to have to deceive you."

"Why the fake engagement?" I said, my heart pounding and my chest hurting as I tried to comprehend what he was telling me.

"Because it was the only way to get the power of attorney through a contract." He sighed. "It was all Nonno's idea."

"He knew I loved you." I sighed. "How could he do this to me? Didn't he know it would just hurt me even more?"

"I think he could see that I loved you as well." TJ gave me a half-smile. "Maybe he was trying to give me a push. See what we could have."

"Yeah, I suppose." I looked away from him, deeply hurt.

"And it worked, Mila. I did come to my senses. I love you more than life itself and I might not have realized that if not for this craziness."

"I suppose." I rubbed my forehead, not sure how I was feeling. "It's a lot to take in, TJ."

"I know." He nodded. "There's something else."

"Oh, God," I groaned. "What now?"

"So, Barbie?" He sighed. "She kinda knows the plan, and she's kinda dating my dad."

"WHAT?" I screamed out loud. "Are you joking me? Fucking Barbie knows?"

"Well, she doesn't know everything." He half-smiled. "She thinks I'm doing this for my dad because I want a seat on the board. She thinks I'm doing it begrudgingly. She doesn't know that Nonno is in on it and she doesn't know that we're way overpaying for the company." He smiled at me. "So while she's gloating, I'm smiling inside."

"Smiling inside?" I raised an eyebrow at him.

"Smiling for the great deal." He sighed. "Not the deception."

"Oh, TJ." I rubbed my forehead. "This is so much to understand and take on. I just don't know how to feel."

"Can you forgive me?" he asked, his eyes worried. "Do you still love me?"

"I can forgive you, TJ. Promise me, there are no more secrets." I looked deeply into his eyes. "Moving forward we have to be honest with each other."

"There are no more secrets," he said, his eyes earnest. "I—I love you more than life itself. You know that. There is nothing I wouldn't do for you. Nothing I wouldn't do to be with you. Everything I do is to protect you. Please always know and remember that."

"I love you, TJ. As long as we are honest with each other, nothing can break us apart."

"So we'll sign the paperwork?" he asked me stiffly and I nodded.

"If that's what Nonno wants, then we'll do it." I sighed. "My parents will kill me, but I trust Nonno with everything. I'm going to kill him when I see him next, though. I can't believe he would keep this a secret from me."

"I think part of it was him hoping we'd get together," TJ said softly. "I think he wants me to take over his role. He wants me to love and protect and guide you. He must have seen how much I loved you from the start."

"I don't need anyone to guide me." I rolled my eyes at him and he laughed.

"Shall we go back to the office?"

"Only if you promise me I can bitch-slap that ho, Barbie."

"You have my blessings." He laughed and we just grinned at each other happily. I felt as if my heart were going to burst with happiness and excitement, but for some reason I still felt a sense of unease and worry. Was everything going too perfectly? Had it all turned around too easily?

Chapter Fourteen

I WENT HOME WHEN TJ went to sign the paperwork in the office. We'd both decided that it would be smarter to let Barbie and his dad still think I was in the dark. If they thought I knew, they might get concerned at the price they were paying and neither of us wanted them to investigate that before the deal went through. I was just about to head to the bathroom when the phone started ringing. My heart started pounding and my head went cold. My clammy hands gripped the phone as I went to answer it, and I dropped it before quickly picking it up and answering.

I knew, before I actually knew it. I'm not sure how. I don't think I'm psychic or anything. But when I got the call, I just knew. I didn't say anything. I just got in my car and drove over to Nonno's.

He was pissed, of course, since he'd told me to wait for him to come and pick me up. I wasn't going to wait for that. I couldn't sit around in the house, just waiting. I didn't even cry on the drive over. I'm proud of myself for that. I had to be strong now. It was just me. Or maybe I'd just cried too much over, TJ. Maybe that had depleted my tears.

"Mila," Cody said, opening the door. His eyes were loving, red, and he opened his arms as he stepped forward.

"What's going on?" I said, feeling like I was playing a part. "Where's Nonno?"

"Mila," he said and I watched as he chewed on his lower lip. His face looked distressed and as I stared at him, it suddenly hit me as to why Sally thought he was cute. He was handsome. And I could say that in a completely unbiased way. I didn't even know why I was thinking about that now. Not after the call.

"Where's Nonno? I need to speak to him."

"He's at the hospital. With Mom and Dad," he said slowly, looking at me carefully.

"Then let's go. He most probably wants to see me."

"He's gone, Mila. I told you." His voice trailed off. "Mom and Dad thought it would be better for you to come here. To be with the photos and his spirit and stuff."

"This isn't funny." I pushed past Cody. "Nonno, where are you? Nonno!" I ran through the house. "This isn't a funny joke, Nonno," I screamed as I ran into the kitchen. "Nonno, come out now." I opened the fridge and the oven and all the cupboards and slammed them. "Nonno, come out now. This isn't funny!" I screamed again and ran into his bedroom. I ran over to the closets and opened them. "Nonno, come out," I shouted. "This isn't funny." Tears started to stream down my face. "Nonno, it's me. It's Mila. Please, stop it." I ran into the bathroom and saw the water in the bathtub, where he must have fallen, and I started screaming and screaming. "Nonno, you can't leave me. Oh, Nonno, you can't leave me. Nonno." I collapsed onto the floor of the bathroom and Cody rushed in and sat next to me.

"Come, Mila. Let's go back into the living room."

"His blood's still on the bathtub." I just stared at him, wailing. "I didn't even know he was sick."

"He didn't tell any of us, Mila." Cody held me close. "We didn't know. He had cancer. He's had it for a while."

"He'd tell me!" I screamed. "He'd tell me because he loves me. I mean the world to him. He would never keep a secret from me. "He loved me," I whispered, my body shaking as Cody held me. "How could he die and not tell me? How could he know he was dying and not tell me? Why would he do this to me?" I muttered into his chest as I sobbed.

We sat there for what seemed like hours and then I stood up and walked into the living room. I tried to smile. I tried to feel happy for the life that he'd had, but I couldn't. I sat down on the couch and waited for Cody to walk into the living room behind me.

"I want to see Nonno," I said quietly. "I want to see him."

"Not today." He shook his head. "He split his head open when he fell. Mom and Dad want him taken care of properly before you see him."

"I want to see him," I said louder. "I need to see him, Cody."

"I know you want to see him." He walked over to me. "But you don't want to see him like this, Mila. You want to see him as the man that you know and remember. He wants you to see him as the man he was."

"How could he leave me?" I chewed on my lower lip. "He wasn't supposed to die. Not now, not with me not even knowing. Not with me not even being there. I didn't even get to say goodbye. I didn't even get to tell him about me and TJ." I chewed on my lower lip as I thought about TJ. It almost felt wrong to be so happy about TJ when I was so distraught over Nonno.

"What about you and TJ?" Cody asked, his eyes narrowing.

"It doesn't matter." I shook my head. "But we're in love, really in love."

"Finally," Cody said with a smile. "It took him a while to figure it out."

"Yeah." I sighed and then looked at Nonno's photo album on the table and picked it up. "I guess he's with Nonna now."

"They're dancing around in Heaven, looking down at us," Cody said as I opened the album and we started looking at the photos of Nonno and Nonna and other family members.

"I can't believe he didn't tell me," I said, tears pouring from my eyes. "I'm going to miss him so much."

"He loved you with everything, Mila. He'll always be here, you know," Cody said and rubbed my back. "He'll always be here, protecting us, like a guardian angel."

"I don't want him to be my guardian angel," I sobbed. "I just want him to be my Nonno."

"TJ," I SAID AS I answered the phone, crying.

"Oh, Mila." He sounded anguished. "I just heard the news. I'm so sorry."

"I can't believe he's gone, TJ. I don't know what I'm going to do. I can't believe it. I don't know how I can survive."

"He fought the cancer as hard as he could, Mila. He tried his hardest. He didn't want to hurt you." TJ's voice was sympathetic. "Where are you? Let me come and be with you. Let me hold your hand. Cry on my shoulder. I want to be there for you."

"How did you know he had cancer?" I whispered. "And how do you know he fought his hardest?" My heart felt cold as I waited for his answer.

"Mila," he said, his voice breaking.

"TJ, answer me.

"Mila, let me come and see you, please."

"Did you know he was dying?" I asked, my heart in my throat. "Did you know Nonno was dying and you didn't tell me?"

"He made me promise not to say anything. He didn't want you living with that fear and dread. He didn't want you to know. He thought the wait would kill you. He thought it would be agony."

"You promised, no more secrets. We promised each other to only tell the truth. You promised me, TJ."

"I couldn't tell you, Mila. I just couldn't."

"I loved him more than anything in the world. You knew that. He died while we were away. I wasn't even here to be with him. I've barely seen him the last month because of you and you knew he was dying."

"Mila, I tried to get you to see him. I wanted to tell you, but Nonno—he didn't want you to know."

"How could you keep that from me, TJ?"

"I love you, Mila. I'm sorry. I didn't mean to hurt you."

"You don't know what love is, TJ. You lied to me again. You have ripped my heart out. I have lost the only man who has loved me more than life itself. How could you do this to me?" And then I threw my phone across the room and watched as it hit the wall and fell to the ground and exploded into a million pieces, just like my heart.

Chapter Fifteen

Mila

THE BEAT OF MY HEART was in perfect symmetry to the sound of the beat of the drum on the radio. I stood there, standing in my room, in the darkness and pressed my hands together. A small cry fell from my lips as TJ's face passed through my mind. I closed my eyes to try and banish his face from my thoughts, but that didn't help. I could only see it bigger, brighter, clearer. I opened my eyes again and walked to my bed slowly. I collapsed down onto the sheets, praying that sleep would take me right away, but of course I wasn't to be so lucky. Emptiness filled me. My heart felt hollow like the inside of the huge conch shell Nonno and I had found on the beach when I was younger. I looked over to the shelf to the right of the bed and stared at the shell that I still treasure so that I could concentrate on something other than TJ. That didn't help. I cried out again as TJ's bright green eyes flashed in my mind and all I could see was the warmth of his smile from a few days ago. My TJ. Oh how I loved this man. Every single inch of him. I just wanted to reach out and touch him, I needed to feel him, wanted that contact. Just one last time. My body shivered on the bed as I lay there alone, tired, weary, cried out.

My heart started to pound as I realized that I could quite possibly die like this. All alone. Heartbroken. More tired than I'd ever felt in my life. My life seemed pointless and hopeless. Life was so incredibly unfair. Why hadn't he loved me enough to tell me about Nonno? Why didn't he care? Couldn't he see that we were made for each other? Couldn't he see that my heart beat for him? Couldn't he see how strong I was? I found my eyes gently closing as my sobs started up again. I grabbed my pillow and held it close to me, imagining it was him. The pain shot through my body as I lay there and a feeling of nausea rose through me. I wasn't going to be okay. Nothing was ever going to be okay again. My heart had shattered into a million pieces and TJ Walker, my soul mate, didn't even seem to care that he was partially responsible, by not telling me that my Nonno was dying.

"I DON'T THINK I HAVE a heart anymore. I can't feel it beating. I can't hear it ticking. I think it's left my body," I sobbed to Sally as she sat on my bed and held me. "I don't think I'm going to be okay ever again. I can barely breathe. I can't think. I just want to die."

"Oh Mila. It's okay. It's going to be okay."

"It's not going to be okay," I cried, my stomach feeling emptier than it ever had. I looked up at her bleakly. "I feel like I mean nothing. I'm nothing. I'm invisible."

"You're not invisible."

"And yet I am. I don't matter."

"You do matter. Mila, you're scaring me."

"I'm sorry, I don't even know what to say. I lost Nonno, and the one person I ever really and truly loved has ripped my heart to pieces."

"TJ didn't mean . . ."

"I can't even hear his name," I sobbed. "I can't even think about him without the pain burning me up inside. I hate him so much. I hate him. I hate him. I hate him. I hate him."

"Oh Mila."

"I'm not waiting for him. I'm not crying for him. I'm not think-ing of him. I don't love him. I don't love him." Then the tears started streaming even more. "Oh, God, I love him so much it hurts."

"Call him, Mila." Sally looked down at me with a worried expression. "Call him and let him know how you feel."

"I don't know how I feel."

"Just speak to him."

"Okay." I nodded finally and grabbed my phone and waited for him to answer.

"Mila?" he asked hopefully and for a second my heart beat just a little bit faster as I heard his voice. Then I quickly banished my momentary happiness.

"Yes, it's Mila."

"It's me, TJ."

"I know. I called you." My voice was stiff and tinged with bitterness.

"Mila, talk to me, please. Tell me what I can do. Tell me what you want."

"We could have had it all," I said, not saying anything else.

"Or we could have had nothing." TJ's voice was sad.

"I loved you."

"Loved? I thought love never died."

"It died."

"So then, maybe it wasn't love."

"You're an ass."

"I'm just saying how it is. If you loved me, past tense, then maybe it wasn't really love."

"Yeah, maybe it wasn't."

"Just lust."

"You wish."

"Infatuation then."

"Yeah, that's it."

"Obsession."

"I'm not obsessed."

"Maybe I was."

"You were?"

"Maybe."

"I see."

"Maybe it hurt too much."

"Being obsessed hurt?"

"No."

"Then what?"

"Being in love." His words were soft now.

"With yourself?"

"No. With someone where the thought of ever having to say goodbye was too hard to handle."

"I see."

"Do you?"

"No."

"Maybe some part of me just knew."

"Knew what?" I was annoyed now.

"It doesn't matter."

"Okay," I said and then looked towards Sally and smiled brightly. "I think I'm going to go now. I've things to do." My heart thudded painfully, but I didn't want him to know just how badly he'd hurt me.

"It doesn't die," he said softly, his voice tinged with a hint of desperation and sadness.

"What doesn't die?"

"Love. If you had really loved me, it wouldn't have died." He paused and I stared at the ceiling for what seemed like an eternity before turning back to the phone. "I wanted to tell you about Nonno, Mila. I really did. I regret it more than anything. But I can't take it back. Please don't give up on me. This is what I was afraid of. This is why I didn't want to love you. This is why I didn't want to let you in. I was scared something like this would happen and you would just walk away. I was scared you'd just give up on us. If you really loved me, you would understand, Mila. You'd know that this was something I couldn't give you. Not without betraying, Nonno. You have to grow up, Mila. You have to understand that you'll be okay. I know you might not love me anymore, but we can still try." He was silent then and so was I.

It was in that moment that I gave up on him, on us, on everything I'd seen in my mind's eye. It was in that moment that I knew that he could never be my one. He, who had turned my world around, didn't get me, didn't understand me, didn't realize that after all these years, he was everything to me. He didn't understand that my love was forever. He couldn't comprehend that I would never not love him anymore. But I knew that I had to try to get over him. The end had come before the beginning and I was finally ready to let go.

Chapter Sixteen

TJ

Dear TJ,

Do you remember the day that you asked me to never forget you? A simple request. I didn't think much of it. We were young then. "Never forget me you said," your eyes bright and hopeful. "Of course, I'd never forget you," I said, and I giggled. I'd never imagined a time when you wouldn't be in my mind. How could I forget the boy who meant so much to me? This was even before I knew what that feeling was. How could I ever forget the man whose smiles and frowns turned my heart upside down? I thought I'd go to my grave waiting for you, if that was how long it took, such was my love.

I gave up today. The pain is too much. My heart is too sore. I can't wait anymore. I don't want to keep falling falling falling into your abyss of a soul. I don't want to remember you. I don't want to see your smiles for anyone, but me. It drives me crazy, wanting you so badly, but not being able to tell you, not being able to love you. I never imagined a longing so cutting, an aching so unfamiliar. I never knew what it was to feel broken in pieces. When you look into my eyes and smile, it still lights up my heart. It still makes me feel like I'm special. How I wish that were true.

So I'm sorry, I can't honor my promise. I can't "never forget" you. I can't do this anymore.

Mila

Dear Mila,

You were wearing a white shirt with a green cardigan. Your hair was pulled back, slightly messy. You had on a soft pink lipstick, light mascara. You were excited because you were going to a concert the next day with Sally and you had good seats. You were dancing around the living room with a water bottle, singing along to some horrible Top-40 song. You stopped abruptly when you saw me standing there watching you. And then you started laughing. And then I started laughing and you threw a couch cushion at me for laughing at you. Even though I told you I was laughing with you. Your eyes narrowed and you glared at me and I laughed some more, my eyes on your lips, wondering for the briefest of seconds what it would be like to kiss you. Then you walked closer to me and hit me on the shoulder and I moved back abruptly, slightly uncomfortable at the touch. Not because I didn't like you, but because it made me feel something electrifying. A wave of worry and disappointment crossed your features for the briefest of seconds when I stepped back. And I knew I'd hurt you. And I hated that. I then reached over, brushed a wisp of hair from in front of your eyes and you grinned at me. And in that moment, in that moment, I knew you were someone special. And I said to you, "Promise me that you'll never forget me and that we'll always be friends." I said that, "if anything ever happens to us and we are ever split by a continent or some unknown situation, I want you to always remember me and to wait, to wait for me to find you, because I would always find you and I would always remember you." And you smiled at me happily and said, "of course, I'd never forget you." And my heart beat then, for what felt like the first time. And I knew that in that moment, I would do anything to keep you in my memory. In my heart. In my soul.

So yes, dear Mila, I remember that moment. I remember every moment. I know it seems like I have an abyss of a soul, but I don't. The hardest part of being me is holding back from you when all I want to do is hold you close for an eternity.

You don't have to honor your promise, but I'll always be here. I'll always remember you and I'll always be here waiting. Waiting for the day when it doesn't have to be this hard.

TJ

Chapter Seventeen

TJ

Two Weeks Later

MY HEART WAS RACING AS I made my way over to Cody's house. He'd told me to come over. He told me that Mila knew I was coming. And yet, I was still unsure and uncertain as to her reaction towards me. What would she say? How would she feel? She'd never responded to my letter. And I hadn't wanted to harass her and bombard her with calls and texts. I was dying to see her. Dying to hear from her, but I knew I'd fucked up. I knew I hadn't been the man she'd needed and now I had to be patient. I'd wait for the rest of my life if that was what I had to do. I wouldn't even mind. I would wait until the day I died, if it meant that my last breath could be spent with her.

I rushed up the stairs to Cody's house and pounded on the door, anxiety killing me.

"Hey," Mila said as she answered the door, her brown eyes friendly but hesitant. I stared at her, taking in all of her beauty. Her long blond hair was flowing down her back, her face looked thinner, her lips trembling slightly as she tried to smile. Her eyes looked into mine hesitantly, shining brilliantly and I just wanted to swoop her into my arms and hold her and kiss her and never let go.

"Hey," I said, my throat dry. I didn't know what to say. She was here, in front of me, as beautiful as ever and I felt like I was a little boy again, unsure and needy. "Cody invited me over," I continued dumbly.

"I know." She nodded. "He's not here." She ushered me in. "I wanted to talk to you."

"Oh?" I said, my body turning cold. "Why?" Fear invaded my soul. Was this when she was going to tell me that she no longer loved me, but she wanted to be friends?

"Because there's something—"

"Wait." I held my hand up. "Before you say anything, I need to talk to you." I knew this was my moment. This was the moment I had to prove myself, once and for all. I was the man. I was the man and I needed her to know that I wanted her. I needed her to know that her love hadn't been in vain. I'd woo her for the rest of her life. I'd chase her. I'd do whatever she wanted me to do. I needed to be her one. I needed her to see I was her soul mate. The one she'd been waiting for forever. I was her forever love. I was the man who had been sculpted to love every inch of her. I was made to love her. Made to please her. Made to make her happy. She needed to know that. She needed to know that I wasn't going away. I'd never give up. Love like ours didn't come easily. Or to everyone. We were the lucky ones and we couldn't just throw that away.

"Okay." She frowned. "Go ahead." She looked at me curiously, her eyes searching mine and I stared back at her, smiling, letting my emotions shine through.

"I wrote this for you." I cleared my throat and started to recite the poem I'd written.

"I loved you for a million years.

And then I met you.

And my love for you was more than my heart.

My heart was more than my soul.

My soul was more than the universe.

The universe was less than my love.

I loved you then.

I love you now.

I love you forever.

Till death do us part.

And then I'll love you for a million years more."

She just stared at me in silence and I cleared my throat. I was embarrassed, but proud of myself. I cleared my throat and spoke again.

"I wrote it because a long time ago, you said your perfect man, your soul mate, would write you love poems. And I wanted to prove to you that I'm your soul mate. Your fated destiny. The one you've been waiting for. The one who was made for you. I know I'm an idiot and an asshole. And I know I have a lot to learn. And I'm not perfect and maybe sometimes I don't act like that guy, but I'm him. I want you to know that I'm him. I want to spend the rest of my life showing you that I'm him. Can I spend the rest of my life showing you how much I love you and want to be with you?" I paused and stared at Mila's face, my breath coming fast. "Say something, please?"

"I love you, TJ Walker." Her eyes were brimming with tears. "These are happy tears, by the way. I love you so much, you don't even know. You are already my perfect man. You will always be my perfect man."

"Are you just saying that?" I said, knowing I would break something if she said yes. My whole body felt like it was going to float away because I was so happy. "Please say you're not just saying that."

"No." She grinned and stepped towards me and gave me a kiss. "Nonno left me a letter. He told me off." She laughed. "He wrote that he knew I would be pissed at you and most probably would stop talking to you. He said he knew I would think you didn't love or trust me enough. He told me that I should be proud to be with a man who loved and respected him enough to uphold his promise. He said that I shouldn't be an idiot and I should be grateful to him for getting us together and to not mess it up." She laughed and touched my face. "I laughed and I cried reading his letter. Oh, TJ, I still hurt so much, but I need you to know—I want you to know—I love you more than anything. I always have. I always will. You are my everything. Nothing can ever part us. You know that, right?"

"I know." I grinned at her and kissed her hard. "I know that we're it. Forever. I don't want you for four weeks, Mila. I want you for the rest of my life. Will you marry me and make me the happiest man in the world?"

"Oh yes, TJ. Oh yes. I'll be your forever wife." And then I kissed her good and hard and promised myself that I would never let her go.

"Do your parents hate me?" I asked her as we just stood there holding hands.

"No." She shook her head. "I think they realized that what Nonno did was the best for everyone. My parents are going to retire. And, well, your dad put Cody in charge of the company."

"I know." I smiled. "I made that happen."

"You did?" She looked at me in surprise.

"Cody is my best friend. He's going to be my brother." I grinned, happy at the thought. "I had to hook him up."

"How did you do that?"

"I've got a few things on my dad." I laughed. "Let's just say, I put all my cards on the table to make sure this deal went through the way I wanted it to."

"Thank you," she said softly. "Thank you for looking out for me and Cody and my parents."

"I never knew what it was to think of someone more than my-self," I said, thoughtfully, needing her to understand how I felt and the depth of my love for her. "I never knew that I could care about someone so much that I would move mountains to make them happy. I would move mountains for you, Mila. I would swim oceans. I would fight a lion, a tiger, and a shark for you. I would walk across the Sahara Desert, battle an army with my bare hands. There is nothing I wouldn't do for you. I wake up every morning and you are the first thing on my mind. Every single morning. And that makes me happy. That makes me want to wake up. Just the thought of you. And at night—at night when I feel alone, or cold, or tired—I just think of your smile. Or your laugh. I close my eyes and just lie there and it makes me feel secure, comforted, warm inside. I've never felt that before. I've never known that love could feel this way. And the best part . . . the best part is that I'm not scared. I'm not scared of it ending or fading away. I'm not scared because I know that true love never dies. I will never not love you, Mila. I will never not want to be the man holding your hand. I will never not be your one."

"I loved you from the first moment I saw you, TJ Walker. I know that sounds weird. I was too young to even know what love was. And I didn't know you. But inside, the second I laid eyes on you, I knew. I've always known. I think Nonno must have known as well. Maybe it was destined in the stars. Maybe we really were carved for each other by some master sculptor. I don't know how it could be. But I've known from the first second that you were mine. I didn't fully understand the depth of my feelings until I got older. And these last few weeks, well, they made me love you even more. I got to know you. I saw your flaws. I saw your weaknesses. I saw the man you were under the facade. And sometimes I hated that guy. Some days I just wanted to cry. But I never wanted to walk away and I never thought, not even for a nanosecond, that I would stop loving you. Because that will never happen. I cannot be me if I don't love you."

"And I cannot be me, if I cannot love you." I grinned at her and pulled a ring out of my pocket. "Will you accept this ring, Mila? Will you marry me? Will you do me the honor of being my wife for eternity?"

Mila's eyes widened and tears streamed down her face, only this time I didn't feel a sense of worry at the waterworks display. "Yes, TJ. There's nothing I'd like more." She leaned forward and kissed me, her eyes glowing as I slid the ring onto her finger.

"What about Cody and Sally?" I winked at her and she grinned.

"Well, yes, I'd like to see them together as well." She laughed. "But that's a matter for another time."

"I know." I laughed and kissed her again. "We'll work our magic and we'll get them together too."

"I sure hope so." She sighed blissfully and gazed up into my eyes lovingly. "I want them to be as happy as we are. I want them to share a love like ours."

"There is no better love than what we have." I kissed her lips lightly. "We have a forever love. We will always be together, flying through the sky, surfing on clouds, singing with the birds and howling in the wind. We'll always be us and I'm not afraid anymore. I'm not afraid of anything."

Thank you for reading Four Week Fiance 2. I am releasing a book for Sally and Cody called, Say You Love Me. Please join my mailing list here to be notified of all my new releases.
http://eepurl.com/bpCvd1

You can also like my Facebook page here (facebook.com/ J.S.Cooperauthor) or email me at jscooperauthor@gmail.com.

Printed in Great Britain
by Amazon.co.uk, Ltd.,
Marston Gate.